KU-274-507

THE SECRET OF OTHELLO

A FISHER KEY ADVENTURE

BARKING & DAGENHAM

906 000 000 64690

Praise for *Mystery of the Tempest*

"Intrigue that will delight genre enthusiasts...a true mystery with something to offer teens of any orientation."
—*Kirkus Reviews*

"Fast, fun, and a great beach read."—Kristin Cashore, *New York Times* bestselling novelist.

"*Mystery of the Tempest* is brilliantly conceived and executed. The characters literally jump off the page and into your heart. A funny, thrilling, authentic young adult novel in the Fisher Key Adventure series. I can't wait for the next installment."
—Julie Anne Peters, author of *Luna* and *Keeping You a Secret*

"Danger, mystery, suspense, romance, conflict, and teen angst woven into a plot that speeds along complete with crackling dialogue—what more could a reader want? You'll be hooked from the tense opening scene, and after you turn the last page, you'll eagerly await the sequel. Sam Cameron's writing is a gift to teens, past and present. Thoroughly enjoyable."
—Lesléa Newman, author of *Heather Has Two Mommies* and *A Letter to Harvey Milk*

By the Author

The Fisher Key Adventures

Mystery of the Tempest

The Secret of Othello

Visit us at www.boldstrokesbooks.com

THE SECRET OF OTHELLO

A FISHER KEY ADVENTURE

by

Sam Cameron

A Division of Bold Strokes Books

2012

LB OF BARKING &
DAGENHAM LIBRARIES

90600000064690	
Bertrams	25/01/2013
AF	£11.50
GAY	

THE SECRET OF OTHELLO: A FISHER KEY ADVENTURE
© 2012 By Sam Cameron. All Rights Reserved.

ISBN 13: 978-1-60282-742-4

This Trade Paperback Original Is Published By
Bold Strokes Books, Inc.
P.O. Box 249
Valley Falls, NY 12185

First Edition: September 2012

THIS IS A WORK OF FICTION. NAMES, CHARACTERS, PLACES, AND INCIDENTS ARE THE PRODUCT OF THE AUTHOR'S IMAGINATION OR ARE USED FICTITIOUSLY. ANY RESEMBLANCE TO ACTUAL PERSONS, LIVING OR DEAD, BUSINESS ESTABLISHMENTS, EVENTS, OR LOCALES IS ENTIRELY COINCIDENTAL.

THIS BOOK, OR PARTS THEREOF, MAY NOT BE REPRODUCED IN ANY FORM WITHOUT PERMISSION.

CREDITS
EDITORS: GREG HERREN AND STACIA SEAMAN
PRODUCTION DESIGN: STACIA SEAMAN
COVER DESIGN BY SHERI (GRAPHICARTIST2020@HOTMAIL.COM)

For Steve and Alex

CHAPTER ONE

The most dangerous woman on Fisher Key leaned toward Steven Anderson with a smile promising all sorts of trouble. He told himself to keep calm. His friends were clustered on a picnic bench nearby, where the parking lot gave way to ocean and a twilight sky. But none of them knew what trouble he was in. He'd have to handle this on his own.

"So, Steven." Melissa Hardy's eyebrows arched provocatively. "Have you decided?"

She was wearing an absurdly tight pink T-shirt. The white straps of her bra peeked out, thin and lacy against her tanned shoulders. Her blond hair hung in a glossy ponytail.

Steven took a deep breath. "Double-scoop hot chocolate with nuts."

She grinned. "You always were a double-scoop kind of guy. Glad to see nothing changes."

Melissa grabbed her metal scoop and leaned down to the ice cream bins. Her family had run the Dreamette Creamery for as long as Steven could remember. His crush on her had started sometime around sixth grade and hadn't diminished at all in the two years she'd been away at the University of Florida.

No women, he reminded himself. For the rest of the summer, he'd sworn off all members of the opposite sex no matter how pretty, how nicely they filled out their T-shirts, or how bright their smiles on a Saturday night.

What a stupid vow to make.

"I hear you're going to become a SEAL," Melissa said. "That's awesome."

"That's the plan." He didn't want to talk about it. Most people on the island didn't know that he'd been rejected and lied about it. The crushing humiliation of being denied over a single vision test still made him squirm. It had been more than a week since his formal waiver request had gone in.

Surely someone had made a decision by now, right?

Melissa stuffed ice cream into the cone. "I'm jealous. You'll be saving the world while I'm stuck in anatomy and physiology."

"I didn't know you were pre-med," he said.

"I want to be a coroner. That way none of them can talk back to you."

He pictured her with hair pulled up in a bun and her blue eyes framed by sexy librarian glasses. She'd wear a tight lab coat and snap on those rubber gloves and oh, boy, if he didn't stop thinking like that he was going to embarrass himself right against the counter.

Melissa rolled the ice cream in chopped walnuts. "You're awfully quiet tonight. I'd almost think you were Denny."

"Denny's not quiet," Steven replied. In fact, sometimes his twin brother never shut up. Lately, all he did was yammer on about going away to the Coast Guard Academy at the end of the month. Steven was so sick of it that he was going to apply duct tape the next time Denny mentioned Swab Summer.

"He's not as talkative as you." Melissa lifted the cone. "I'm not used to a Steven Anderson whose mouth isn't moving."

A blush warmed his face. "It still moves."

"Good." She gave him that bright smile again. "Here's your ice cream. All ready for your mouth."

As he dug for his wallet, a southbound blue SUV pulled into the lot and parked near the trash cans. He didn't recognize it, or the two men who got out. But that wasn't unusual. The Dreamette was right on the Overseas Highway. Tourists on their way down to Key West or up to Miami often stopped at the sight of the old-fashioned sign. The two men halted a few feet from the SUV to check their phones.

Steven handed Melissa his money. She rang it up and asked, "So what are you doing until you go away to boot camp?"

"Nothing. Just hanging out."

"Me, too," she replied. "Unless I'm working here, I'm just hanging out at home. Totally bored."

No women, he reminded himself. He hadn't called Jennifer or Kelsey. He'd kept himself from flirting with pretty guests at the Fisher Key Resort, where he spent his days in the lifeguard chair. He didn't even think about girls while he was in the shower—no, that was silly, *of course* he did. He was taking two or three showers a day.

"Sucks to be bored," he said.

Her smile dimmed. "Yeah. It does."

Steven clamped his jaw shut. He wouldn't ask her out on a date. He wouldn't think about his lifelong quest to get her naked. He wouldn't, wouldn't, wouldn't—

"Or we could be bored together," he said, and instantly regretted it.

The grin came back, wide and lovely. Her lip gloss shimmered.

"That sounds like a much better plan," Melissa agreed. "Call me and we'll figure something out."

The two men from the SUV came up from behind Steven and studied the menu board. He trudged off, mentally kicking himself. Denny was going to gloat like a madman when he found out about Steven's date. Then again, maybe they could do something that wasn't technically a date. They could talk about college, for instance. About coroners. About something that had nothing to do with kissing or sliding his hand under her bra—

"You look like someone killed your dog," Eddie Ibarra said when Steven reached the picnic tables. Eddie was Steven's best friend, or used to be. It was hard to say these days.

Steven sat down. "I don't have a dog."

"I have four dogs," said Robbie Gerstein, who had played on the high school baseball team with Steven until graduation last month. They also worked together as lifeguards at the Fisher Key Resort. "One of them's pregnant. You can have any puppy you want."

"He's going away, idiot," Eddie said, even though he knew the truth about Steven. "He's not stuck here like us."

Robbie said, "I'm going away, too."

"Key West Community College is not going away," Eddie mocked.

"At least I'm going somewhere," Robbie retorted, which made Eddie slug him in the arm.

Laughter rang out from down by the water. Some girls he knew were pitching rocks into the waves and sharing a bottle from a paper bag. Above them, the sky shaded from gold to blue. No moon yet, but stars had begun to glitter. One looked bright enough to be a planet.

Actually, that bright dot was moving. A plane, then.

But no, moving too fast to be a plane. Streaking, bright and swift.

"Shooting star!" one of the girls exclaimed.

His mouth full of double chocolate ice cream, watching the light fall, Steven felt queasy. With dead certainty he knew he'd be sitting in this exact same spot next summer. And the summer after that, and the summer after that one, stuck in place, never moving on. If the Navy didn't take him he had no backup plan. He'd been so stupid, assuming he could just have what he wanted and worked toward for so many years.

The meteor—because that's what falling stars were, just hunks of rock on fire—slammed into the ocean. The girls clapped and Eddie said, "So what?"

A noise made Steven glance over to the Dreamette counter. Almost too late, he saw one of the men grabbing a bag from Melissa. Her smile was gone, replaced by terror.

"Call nine-one-one," Steven said, thrusting his ice cream toward Eddie.

"What?" Eddie asked.

The men sprinted back toward their SUV.

"Tell them two men just robbed the Dreamette!" Steven said, and ran for his truck.

CHAPTER TWO

D enny Anderson stepped inside the chilly, opulent lobby of the Fisher Key Resort and immediately stopped. Two women in cocktail dresses glided by, on the arms of men wearing dark sports jackets. Jazz music floated out of the lounge, where rich tourists had crowded around the bar. Denny was suddenly and absolutely certain he looked like a scruffy beach rat in his khaki shorts, brown shirt, and sandals. He should have worn a suit. Or a suit and tie. Shoes with actual laces in them.

Twenty-three days until he left Fisher Key for the Coast Guard Academy, his first official date with another guy, and he was screwing it all up.

Maybe he should just go home.

His phone buzzed with a message from Brian: *where r u?*

Denny didn't answer. He was too busy thinking about turning around, getting back in his dad's car, and going home. But it was already getting dark out, and he didn't want to make Brian wait, and really now, why wasn't there a 1-800-Tell-Me-What-Gay-Guys-Do?

Besides. Twenty-three days. He wasn't going to be the only virgin at Swab Summer, thank you very much.

Denny took a deep breath and walked to the elevator.

"Hey, Steven!" That was Marcus Sanders, standing behind the front counter in a spiffy green uniform. Marcus had ranked third in the high school class, right behind Denny. He was waiting to go off to the University of Miami in the fall. "What are you doing here?"

"Um, nothing." Denny didn't correct Marcus's mistake. Half the time, people couldn't tell him and Steven apart. "Picking up a date."

"Someone I know?"

"No." And now Denny was screwed, wasn't he, because he couldn't pretend to be Steven and walk out with Brian. He couldn't even be himself and walk out with a guy on his arm. Only a few people knew that he was gay. "I mean, not a date. A friend. We're going to pick up our dates."

Marcus looked puzzled. "You have a friend staying here?"

Denny pictured the hole he was digging for himself. Six feet deep and getting deeper every second. "It's a long story."

"If you say so. Hey, how'd that thing with the jewel thieves turn out?"

"They weren't exactly jewel thieves," Denny said, but that was an even longer story—how Brian's stepdad had stolen diamonds from his own family, and how Brian's house had been burned down, and oh, yes, his parents were divorcing and his mother wasn't taking things well.

"Whatever they were," Marcus said. "When are you going away to the SEALS?"

"I'm not—" Denny shook his head. He had no good way to end that sentence, either. "Never mind."

The front desk phone rang, enabling Denny's escape into the elevator. When the mirrored doors slid shut he again feared that he was maybe underdressed. And wasn't he supposed to bring something? When Steven picked up girls on a date, he brought flowers. Denny had no idea if gay guys brought each other flowers. Maybe chocolates. Maybe those chocolate-covered strawberry basket things?

He was so bad at this gay thing.

For the next thirty seconds, as the elevator glided upward, he obsessed over the part in his hair, the razor nick on the side of his chin, and the tiny red zit trying to pop out on the bridge of his nose. He turned sideways, sucked in his stomach, turned back. He tucked his shirt in, but that didn't help. He pulled it out again.

The elevator doors slid open. Brian had said they were staying in suite at the far end of the hallway. After the fire they'd moved into a rental home, but Mrs. Vandermark didn't like the isolation and they moved again a few days later. *Nice to have money*, Denny thought. Except money hadn't made Brian's stepdad happy at all. It had just made him more greedy.

Denny reached the suite and pushed the doorbell. He stuck his hands in his pockets. Best to look casual. But not too casual, maybe, so he slid them out again. He folded them across his chest, but that looked stern. Clasped them behind his back. No, too military.

You are such a dork, Steven's voice said in his head.

The door swung open. Brian stood on the other side, looking as cute and adorable as ever with his glasses and shaggy hair. He was dressed in a rumpled T-shirt and wrinkled shorts.

"Hi," Brian said, smiling, but the smile was forced. "I sent you a message."

"I was downstairs," Denny said. And this was awkward, too, because was he supposed to kiss Brian hello? Shake his hand in a manly but affectionate way? "Just getting into the elevator."

"You're right on time."

"That's me," Denny said. "Punctual."

From inside the suite came Mrs. Vandermark's voice. "Is that Denny? Bring him in. You know we can't leave the door open."

Brian stepped aside to let Denny inside. The walls were dark green and the entryway floor tiled in marble. The air-conditioning was so cold that Denny swore he could see his breath. The foyer led past a kitchenette to a living room decorated in shades of coral and green. Mrs. Vandermark was sitting on an oversized sofa, watching TV. She smiled at him, but her smile wasn't much better than Brian's.

"Hello, Denny," she said. She was wrapped up in a blue terrycloth bathrobe and sipping white wine from a glass. "You look very handsome tonight."

"Thanks," Denny replied. "This is a nice suite."

"It'll do." Mrs. Vandermark's gaze drifted back to the TV. "Not quite like home."

Brian tugged on Denny's arm. "I'll show you my room."

The feel of Brian's fingers—warm, electric—almost made Denny shiver. He followed him down another hallway to a neat bedroom with dark brown furniture and a giant bed. Books were piled on the bedside table and next to the TV. Brian read books like other people drank water. Right now he was in a Stephen King phase, with *Duma Key* sitting on top of *Bag of Bones* and *Under the Dome*.

But it was the bed that really snagged Denny's attention. The fluffy pillows and chocolate brown comforter looked luscious enough to fall into. The big ticking clock in his head flashed a bright red message: 23 DAYS, DENNY! He and Brian could get a lot done on that bed in twenty-three days—if they had some privacy.

Brian closed the door. "Mom's right. You look good."

"You look good, too," Denny said, because it was true—despite his wrinkled clothes, Brian was the best thing that Denny had seen all day.

Brian grinned and leaned forward. "Liar."

That was definitely a cue for a kiss. Which Denny could do, yes, because he might be inexperienced, but he was motivated. Brian's lips were warmer than he remembered, and tasted like coffee and toothpaste, and they made Denny want to push him backward onto that wide, wonderful bed—

From the living room Mrs. Vandermark called out, "Don't forget to ask Denny what he wants from room service."

Brian stepped back apologetically. "Okay, Mom!"

"Doesn't she know we're going out?" Denny asked.

"Yeah, about that." Brian squared his shoulders. "I don't think

I can leave her alone tonight. She's been on the phone all day with lawyers, and she's already on her second bottle of wine."

Denny said, "Oh," and nothing else.

Brian adjusted his glasses. "I'm really sorry. I thought it'd be okay, but what if she passes out? There's no one here to help her but me."

Denny tried to sound reasonable. "She's not going to pass out. She'll probably just go to sleep early."

"She could hit her head or vomit and breathe it in," Brian insisted. "We'd come back and she'd be dead and it would be my fault."

This wasn't an argument Denny could win. He couldn't even bring himself to make Brian feel guilty about it, because, really, wouldn't Denny do the same thing? When your heartbroken and depressed mom needed you, the only decent thing to do was ditch your date and stick around. Brian was a loyal kind of guy, which was something else Denny really liked about him.

But still. Twenty-three days.

"Could you say something instead of stare at me?" Brian asked.

"Sure," Denny replied. "I mean, yes. I get it."

Brian's shoulders relaxed. "Okay. Thanks. I mean, you can stick around. I want you to. We can order from room service and watch TV and maybe she'll go to bed early, okay?"

That was how Denny ended up sitting in an armchair, eating baked chicken and green beans from the resort kitchen, watching not-very-good sitcoms. Mrs. Vandermark steadily drank her wine but didn't say much. She didn't seem upset. Numb, maybe. Denny could empathize, because he was feeling a little numb himself and he didn't even have the benefit of alcohol.

Brian tried to play host, clearing away their dishes and refilling drinks, but he was obviously anxious. Mrs. Vandermark fell asleep against his shoulder sometime around ten o'clock. Brian said, "Mom," and nudged her awake.

"I'm so tired," she murmured, sounding like a young child.

"I'll tuck you in," Brian said.

They were gone for several minutes. Denny remained in the living room. He muted the TV and listened to the distant murmur of their voices, the words indistinguishable. When Brian came back, he looked tired and depressed.

"Sorry." He flopped down on the sofa. "It was a bad day."

"I should go home," Denny offered.

Brian frowned. "I was going to say you should come sit next to me."

That was definitely a better idea. Denny moved over and sat next to him, but he didn't know what he was supposed to do next. Hold hands? Snuggle? Maybe they could move right to the more kissing part, followed by Denny losing his virginity.

"You look like someone about to get run over by a truck," Brian said. "Relax."

"I am relaxed," Denny said hastily. "I'm just not sure."

"Of what?"

"What we're supposed to do."

"We're not supposed to do anything." Brian turned to him so that their knees were bumping. On the silent TV, some reality game show had come on. Contestants in yellow hazmat suits were lining up to cross a rope bridge over a vat of green slime. Brian asked, "Didn't you go on dates with girls or anything? Just to have fun?"

"Sort of."

"Did you ever kiss a girl?"

"I'd rather kiss you," Denny said, honestly.

"We can do more kissing," Brian promised. He reached over and took Denny's right hand. "And later, more stuff, when it feels right."

Denny watched Brian's fingers thread through his own. Hand-holding was kind of weird, but not unpleasantly so. "How much later?"

Brian sounded amused. "Why? Are you on a deadline?"

On the TV, a female contestant fell into the slime.

Denny replied, "No. I mean, kind of. You know that I'm going away in three weeks."

Brian's gaze was intense. "And then what? We're done?"

"No! But I'll be in training for seven weeks, and then the semester starts. I don't know if I'll be able to get away. And you'll be in Boston and you'll have your own schedule." Denny tried to sound casual, but he suspected he was failing. "We don't have a lot of time."

Brian pulled his hand free. Denny wanted to grab it back.

"So this is just something on a checklist?" Brian asked. "Something you want to accomplish before you go away to Connecticut?"

"No!" Denny insisted, although sort of, yes. Summer training at the academy was going to be hard enough without the big invisible "Virgin" stamp on his forehead.

Brian took a deep breath. "Okay, listen. We've only known each other for two weeks. I like you a lot, and I'd say that even if you hadn't saved my life. I really want to see where this goes. But I can't promise anything before you go away."

"Anything at all?" The entire list in Denny's head was beginning to evaporate. It was a detailed list, augmented by online research and lots of years of frustration. It came with illustrations and annotations and milestones—

Brian's gaze jerked past Denny's shoulder to where Mrs. Vandermark had appeared. She was wearing a flimsy white nightgown that revealed more than Denny wanted to see.

"Did I take my medicine?" she asked Brian. "I don't remember."

Brian stood up. "Come on, Mom. Let's get you back to bed."

He steered her back to her room, leaving Denny alone on the sofa with only twenty-three days and that big blinking calendar in his head.

CHAPTER THREE

Rain started to pour down on Denny's drive home. Wind whipped through the pine trees and oaks. Sudden squalls were pretty common over the Florida Keys, especially in summertime, but he slowed down and took extra care crossing the Overseas Highway. His dad wouldn't be happy with a dent in the car.

At home, he parked next to Dad's patrol car and made a mad dash inside. He only got halfway drenched. Inside, the house smelled like fried steak and onions. Dad and Steven were eating a very late dinner at the scratched kitchen table. Dad was in the middle of what sounded like a stern lecture.

"—leave it to the professionals," he was saying. "Someone could have been hurt, and that someone includes you."

"No one got hurt, Dad," Steven said around a mouthful of steak.

"Could have," Dad repeated.

Denny shook water out of his hair. "What did he do now?"

"Nothing," Steven said.

Dad said, "Chased two criminals all the way to Islamorada."

"Didn't chase!" Steven protested. "Followed at a reasonable speed until Dad caught them. Otherwise they'd be in Miami by now."

"With two hundred and thirteen dollars of stolen money," Dad snorted. "Hardly worth your life."

"My life was never in danger." Steven stabbed a chunk of steak with his fork. "How was your date, Denny?"

Dad looked at him, too. "Go like you planned?"

"I don't want to talk about it," Denny said.

Steven smirked. "He didn't put out?"

Dad shot him a disapproving look. "That's the first thing you think about, Steven?"

"It's always the first thing he thinks about," Denny said. "And the last thing. Pretty much the only thing, day and night. Have you seen the water bill lately?"

Steven burped. "Not fair. I think a lot about food, too."

"Your mother would be so pleased to hear about your intellectual depth," Dad said dryly. "By the way, she called and said stay out of trouble. She'll be back on Monday with Aunt Riza in tow."

Denny pulled off his wet shirt and hid a grimace. Aunt Riza was smart and loving, but also the nosiest, bossiest family member they had. She lived in Miami along with their other Cuban relatives but came down once a year to wreak havoc in their lives, like a hurricane.

Speaking of stormy weather, thunder cracked overhead and more rain slammed into the windows. The lights flickered but steadied again.

"Better find your flashlights," Dad said.

By the time they all went to bed, the storm had tapered off to an occasional drizzle. Denny tossed and turned for a while, thinking about Swab Summer. He wasn't worried about the physical aspects— running and push-ups and drills. He was sure, too, that he could handle the mental aspects of being ordered around, broken down, and built back up again. But he was worried that the upperclassmen would take one look at him and know his innermost heart: fag, they'd say, and once the rumor started it couldn't be quenched.

He dreamt he was lost in the drafty halls of the academy

barracks. Coast Guard cadets watched him from the shadows, whispering and leering. Not just gay, but also a virgin, a loser virgin who'd never been touched or loved—

An enormous ripping noise jerked him out of sleep. Denny blinked at the ceiling in confusion, his pulse pounding.

"What was that—" he started to ask.

Thunder outside, a flash of lightning, and then something enormous smashed through the ceiling. Denny didn't get to finish his question at all.

❖

Steven had no idea why he was on the floor, surrounded by soggy leaves and plaster chunks. Was that a tree just a few feet over his head? Lightning flashed beyond the branches, followed by annoyingly loud thunder. Rain drizzled down on his bare chest and legs and his heart jackhammered like a crazy thing. He was too young to have a heart attack, right?

"What?" he demanded, because he thought Denny was nearby and had asked him a question. "What happened?"

Thunder drowned out half of Denny's reply.

"—and it fell in!"

"What fell in?" Steven asked crossly. Sometimes Denny didn't make any sense at all.

"The tree!" Denny answered. "And the ceiling."

Something pounded on wood near Steven. A fist on their door, accompanied by Dad's frantic voice.

"Steven! Denny!" Dad shouted. "Answer me!"

A beam of light cut through the darkness. Denny's flashlight played over their room. Much of the ceiling was gone, smashed in by a turkey oak tree. The destruction was pretty awesome, except for the fact everything Steven owned was crushed or getting ruined by water.

Steven said, "I think that tree fell on us."

"No kidding." Denny was barely visible through the branches, stuck somewhere between his bed and the window. "Dad! We're okay!"

Steven wasn't 100 percent sure about that. His heart was still racing, and his legs and arms were tingling, and he was shivering even though it wasn't very cold. Meanwhile, that red stuff on Denny's forehead probably wasn't ketchup.

"You're hurt," Steven said.

Denny swiped at the blood. "It's fine. You?"

"Nothing's broken."

"The fire department's on its way!" Dad said through the door. "Can you open the door?"

Denny aimed the flashlight at the frame. Part of the enormous trunk had landed on it, and another big chunk was blocking it. The map of the Florida Keys that had hung on the door for years and years was nothing but shredded strips.

"We need a chain saw," Steven said.

"How about the window?" Dad asked.

Denny pushed past some branches and leaves. Steven couldn't see exactly what he was doing, but he heard some cursing.

"Maybe if I had a machete I could get to it," Denny said.

"Just stay put," Dad advised. "We'll get you out."

Steven heard the first sirens in the distance. He dragged a wet pillow off his bed and wriggled around until he could lean against it and the wet wall. "Good thing Mom's not here. She'd be freaking out."

"Dad can freak out for both of them," Denny said. "Where's your phone?"

"Are you going to call her?"

"Of course not. I just want to know what time it is. And you can use it as a flashlight, idiot."

"Oh." Steven groped around on the bed. He usually kept it near his head when he slept, but it wasn't there. He used both hands to pat down the floor. He found one sneaker, an empty soda can, what felt like a dirty dinner plate, and some ruined paperbacks. Military thrillers, all of them. His fingers closed in on a metal rectangle. The small white screen lit up and made him squint.

"It's four fifteen," he said.

"Let me see," Denny said.

Steven passed it through the branches. "Where's yours?"

"In tiny pulverized pieces."

"You broke another one?" Steven snickered. Denny's last two phones had been either smashed or sunk during the case about Brian's dad. The phone before that had been run over by a truck while they were solving the Gas'n'Go robberies. At this rate, Steven might as well forgo the SEALs and just open a cell phone store for Denny alone.

"Shut up," Denny suggested. He punched numbers into the keypad.

"I thought you weren't going to call anyone."

"I'm just checking on Brian." Denny waited, glaring at the screen. "No service."

The fire engine sirens were much louder now, accompanied by what sounded like the island ambulance. Steven knew many of the people who worked emergency services in the Middle Keys. He hoped this rescue didn't take long. It was kind of embarrassing, being trapped in his own bedroom by a tree.

Maybe thinking the same thoughts, Denny said, "I hope this doesn't end up on the front page of the newspaper."

Steven settled down to wait. "I hope they bring breakfast."

CHAPTER FOUR

B rian almost didn't answer his phone. He was dead tired, and the bed was way too soft, and when he slitted one eye open, he could see that it wasn't even fully daylight yet. It should be a crime for anyone to call you before dawn, especially on a Sunday morning. But the phone kept ringing, and maybe it was important. He fumbled for the Answer button.

"Hello?" he croaked out.

"It's Sean," said a hurried voice. Sean Garrity, who worked with Denny at the Bookmine. "You better get over to Denny and Steven's house."

Brian sat upright. "What's wrong?"

"You'll see! You can't miss it. And they're okay, but still stuck."

Brian pulled on some clothes, scribbled a note for his mother, and grabbed her keys. His own car was still being repaired after the accident in Islamorada. On the drive over to Denny's side of the island he saw several tree branches that had been torn down by the storm. Crews were working on phone and power lines. At least the clouds had cleared out, even if the air was still wet and heavy.

Three fire trucks blocked the road at the Anderson house, with an ambulance, two police cruisers, and an electric company truck nearby. Brian parked and approached the house with a giant lump in his throat. A tree had landed exactly where Denny and Steven's room was. If they'd been there when it happened, if they'd been crushed—

But, no, Sean had said they were okay. Brian clung to that.

Rescuers were attacking the tree with chain saws. Captain Anderson was crouched at one window. A rusty air conditioner lay in the scraggly grass behind them.

"Hold up," said one of the policemen when Brian tried to walk closer.

"It's okay, Norman." That was Sean, who broke free from a knot of bystanders. "This is Brian. I called him."

The cop, a tall skinny guy with glasses, said, "Why don't you call the entire island, Sean? Maybe go blog about it, too?"

"Ignore him, he's my cousin," Sean said. "Come on."

They approached the house, careful to keep out of the rescuers' way.

"They're really okay?" Brian asked.

"Apparently, yeah. But Denny won't come out until they get Steven out, too."

"Why? What's wrong with Steven?"

Sean waved his hand. "Nothing. Denny's just being stubborn."

Of course he is. Brian pushed down a sigh of exasperation and surveyed the rest of the property. Aside from the tree, the house looked relatively undamaged. The pier was fully intact and Denny's boat, the *Sleuth-hound*, looked unharmed as well. The lagoon was calm but farther out, the blue-green waves were still choppy from the storm.

"So how'd your date go last night?" Sean asked, a glint in his eyes.

Brian was glad no one was close enough to overhear. Sean and Brian had been openly gay for years. Denny wasn't ready to tell everyone about himself. It was illegal for Coast Guard cadets to be homosexual, even if some lawmakers were talking about repealing Don't Ask, Don't Tell.

"It was okay," Brian said.

"That's it?" Sean asked. "Just okay? Where'd you go?"

"Not far. Isn't there anything we can do to help?"

"Not unless you can make thousands of pounds of wet wood magically go away," Sean said.

For a long time they stood in the grass, watching while firefighters cut at the tree from ladders and a bucket lift. Some others in the house passed chunks of trunk and branches out through windows. The crowd of bystanders grew larger—friends and neighbors who wanted to help, but also people just recording the rescue on their phones. Brian hated that. Denny and Steven were entitled to a little privacy, weren't they?

Kelsey Carlson rushed up to them, her clothes wrinkled and her hair in a messy ponytail. Until very recently, she'd been Steven's girlfriend. Brian wasn't sure of all the details of their breakup, exactly, but the worry on her face was real.

"How are they?" she asked.

"Stuck," Sean said.

Kelsey bit one of her fingernails. "You'd think they could at least stay out of trouble while they were asleep."

The sun was fully up now, and Brian was getting sweaty standing in the grass. Tiny insects irritated his ankles. Sean said, "I'm going to go get some iced coffee. You want something?"

"No," Brian said. "I'll stay here."

Sean had been gone for about fifteen minutes when Captain Anderson said, "Okay, now, careful!" and helped one of the twins climb over the windowsill. Steven or Denny—it was hard to tell— was wearing a fireman's yellow coat and not much else. Captain Anderson squeezed him hard for a minute.

"That's Steven," Kelsey said.

Brian wasn't sure, but when the twin looked past his father and saw Brian on the grass, his face lit up. The chill that had been hanging around Brian warmed right up.

"No," Brian said, swamped with relief. "Denny."

Denny said to his father, "I'm fine. Not a scratch."

"Then what's this?" Captain Anderson asked, touching his forehead. "Nice bump."

Denny shied away from the touch. "I want to wait."

"And I want you to get checked out." Captain Anderson steered him toward the waiting paramedics. "Police orders."

Brian and Kelsey met them at the tailgate of the ambulance. One of the paramedics wrapped a blood pressure cuff around his arm while the other examined his forehead. Denny grinned at Brian and said, "Pretty exciting, huh?"

"That's one way of putting it," Brian agreed. He wanted to wrap his arms around Denny, to squeeze him tight and feel him breathing. He wanted to kiss him, too, and then yell at him for scaring him. But he knew Denny wouldn't want that in front of all these people. All he could do was stand close by and keep his hands still.

Sean joined them, a big cup of coffee in hand. "Think of the odds! Your house gets smashed in and you don't."

"I'd rather not think about that at all, thanks," Captain Anderson said, one hand on Denny's shoulder.

Kelsey asked, "How's Steven?"

"Bored," Denny said. "And he wants a bagel."

Captain Anderson almost laughed. He looked shaken up, Brian decided. Nearly losing both your sons in a freak accident could do that to a guy.

"I better go check on him," Captain Anderson said. "Denny, stay here or you're grounded."

"So not fair," Denny muttered.

Sean asked, "What's it like inside?"

Denny frowned, "Like a big tree smashed everything I own. Everything I was going to take to the academy. My books, my laptop—"

Brian put his hand on Denny's shoulder. "Stuff that can be replaced, okay? Trust me. I know."

Denny nodded. "Okay."

The paramedics didn't seem too worried about Denny's bump, especially since he said he wasn't nauseated or dizzy. Brian thought he might lie if it meant sticking around until Steven got out, but Denny seemed sincere enough. By the time the paramedics were done cleaning the cut, Steven was being helped out through the bedroom window. He, too, was wearing a fireman's coat. He pounded his dad on the back and flashed a cocky grin.

"Can't even get killed by a big falling tree," he said.

Kelsey murmured, "Egotist."

Captain Anderson hugged Steven as tightly as he had Denny, and then brought him to the ambulance as well. Kelsey threw her arms around Steven so hard he staggered a little.

"I was worried," she said.

"Piece of cake." Steven disentangled her with a flash of awkwardness. "The hardest part was keeping Denny calm."

"You were the one freaking out when the chain saws started," Denny said.

Steven sat on the tailgate. "Tell any lie that makes you feel better, Miss Screamypants."

Brian decided that if there was any truth to the situation, it was something they'd keep quiet between them. As an only child he didn't understand much about brothers, and not a lot at all about twins. He had figured out, however, that with these two you couldn't always count on what one of them was saying, and you couldn't always discount it, either.

The paramedics pronounced both twins fine. The on-duty firefighters returned to their trucks but a sizable number of volunteers remained to help with the cleanup and to string tarps over the ruined part of the roof. Denny and Steven both wanted to help, but their father vetoed the idea. Instead, Captain Anderson studied the house and sighed.

"I guess we'll be living in a tent until it all gets fixed up," he said.

"Dad," Steven and Denny both complained.

"What?" Captain Anderson raised both eyebrows. "You like camping. You love spending overnight on islands."

Steven said, "Overnight, yeah. Not for weeks and weeks with no running water in the middle of summer."

Captain Anderson scratched the side of his head. "The insurance might cover a motel."

"A motel," Denny said dubiously.

"If you have a better idea, now's the time to volunteer it," Captain Anderson said.

Denny didn't look at Brian at all. Brian thought about inviting him to stay with him and his mom, but would she agree? Besides, he wasn't sure Denny would enjoy that. Mom was having a hard time with things, as evidenced by the ruined date night, and it might be too much to ask Denny to move into all that drama.

Steven said, "Nathan Carter's boat! He asked me to look after it while he's in the hospital. I'm sure he wouldn't mind if we moved on board."

"Mom's not going to want to live on a boat," Denny said. "How about the apartment over the Bookmine? It's full of junk, but we could clear it out."

Kelsey said, "I'm sure my dad would let you sleep in our guest room, Steven."

Steven lifted his chin stubbornly. "The boat is perfect."

They were still arguing over which option was better when a police sergeant approached, a report in hand. Brian didn't recognize him, but his name tag said *H. Martin*.

"There's a tree on your house, Greg," he said.

"I noticed," Captain Anderson said. "What's that?"

Sergeant Martin handed over the paper. "Just thought you'd like to know. NASA lost a satellite last night. Some chunk of equipment dropped into the ocean."

Steven perked up. "I saw it! Like a shooting star."

"In your dreams," Denny said.

"No, really," Steven insisted.

"What does NASA want us to do?" Captain Anderson asked.

Martin said, "Nothing. Keep an eye out."

"I bet it's a top-secret spy satellite," Steven said. "I could find it for them."

Denny elbowed him. "You're going to be too busy helping me clean out the apartment."

"We don't need an apartment when we have Carter's boat," Steven retorted.

"Tent," Captain Anderson said. "Right here, on the lawn. One big happy family. Because you're crazy if you think I'm letting you out of my sight for even a single minute."

CHAPTER FIVE

In the end, it took begging, logic, and a stroke of good luck to save the day. Steven tried the begging ("Dad, come on, Denny goes away in three weeks and you want him to live in a tent?"). Dad looked sympathetic but unmoved. Denny tried the logical approach ("Dad, we're eighteen years old! That's old enough to live on our own, right?"), but Dad didn't go for that, either.

"Camping will be fun," Dad insisted. "Just like when you were kids."

When they hauled the family tent out of the shed and spread it on the ground, good luck struck. Green mold covered most of the fabric and something had been chewing on the netting.

Dad blinked at the damage. "Okay, plan B. We'll all move into the apartment over the Bookmine."

Steven saw his opening. "It's tiny up there, Dad. We don't even know if the plumbing still works. I'm telling you, Nathan Carter's boat is much better."

"Except that Aunt Riza gets seasick," Denny said.

Steven had forgotten about that. "Okay, so Dad and Mom and Aunt Riza take the apartment, and Denny and I move onto the boat, and everyone's happy."

Dad looked away from the tent at the volunteers still clearing away the tree debris. His forehead was turning red under the steady sunlight, and his clothes were sweaty and grimy. "All right. Get Carter on the phone."

Carter was in physical therapy, so Steven had to leave a message. A half hour later he called back and talked to Dad on the speakerphone.

"Sure, take the boat," Carter said. "I trust the boys. Sorry about your house."

"Thanks, Nathan," Dad replied. "How's things up there?"

Carter huffed. "Fine, except for overprotective mother hens who should go back to the FBI and leave me alone."

In the background, Agent Garcia said, "I heard that!"

Sean, Kelsey, Brian and some other friends volunteered to help the twins move, but there wasn't much worth salvaging. Their laptop had a big crack in it, the TV was a total loss, and their books had turned into soggy lumps of pulp. They grabbed some clothes that needed to be laundered, managed a milk crate each of small stuff, and by lunchtime were sitting on the deck of Carter's old fishing boat, the *Idle*. Sean and Brian had made a sandwich run for everyone. Steven happily dug into an oversized steak and cheese sub with onions and peppers. He felt bad about the house, but living on a boat? *Totally* worth enjoying.

"You're not eating," Brian said to Denny.

Denny poked at his French fries. He tossed one to a seagull on the dock, and a dozen more started clamoring for their share. "Sure I am."

Brian frowned. Steven studied his brother. Dad had told him to keep an eye on that bump on Denny's head, but Steven thought his brother's moroseness had nothing to do with a headache. Almost everything that Denny had been packing for the Coast Guard Academy was either wet or ruined—socks, T-shirts, toiletries, photos, even all that study material he'd downloaded.

"There's plenty of time to replace your stuff," Steven said.

"Yeah." Denny threw another French fry. "I know."

"The important thing is that no one got killed." Kelsey dug into a blue cooler she'd filled with ice and soda. "It could be a lot worse."

Steven appreciated the sentiment, but he wasn't sure why Kelsey was hanging around. It wasn't as if they'd gotten back together. She'd let him borrow her father's boat back when Denny and Brian were stranded on Mercy Key, but she was still mad that he'd slept with Jennifer O'Malley. Or at least she should be. That had been a kind of rotten thing to do. Yet she'd given him a big hug this morning and kept looking at him fondly.

No women, he reminded himself.

Brian's phone rang. Steven had heard it buzzing before, but Brian had ignored it until now. "I'm right here," Brian said when he answered, and then he walked away for some privacy. When he came back he said to Denny, apologetically, "I have to go home."

Sean stood up. "I should go, too. Robin's been at the Bookmine by herself all day."

"The store!" Denny exclaimed. "I totally forgot."

"We can take care of it," Sean promised. "Completely under control."

Brian reached out as if to touch Denny's arm, then stopped himself. "I'll call you later, okay?"

Denny nodded. "Yeah. Okay."

Something passed between them that Steven couldn't quite figure out. He was glad Brian had come over. He still wasn't sure, based on Denny's answers about their date, whether they were officially boyfriend-and-boyfriend now, or just friends waiting to see what came next.

Not that Steven had any interest in Denny's love life, but if Denny ended up moping about this relationship for the next three weeks, Steven would have to throw him overboard.

After lunch, Kelsey dropped Denny and Steven back at their house. She had to leave after that, and Steven was relieved she didn't try to give him a good-bye kiss. Instead she said, "Call me if you need anything," and Steven said he would, though he probably wouldn't.

"Are you two getting back together?" Denny asked as they crossed the yard.

"No. Absolutely not," Steven said.

The house looked positively peaceful now that the fire department and police cruisers had left. An electrician was working on the damaged mast and wires. Most of the fallen oak tree had been piled up nearby, waiting to be mulched or hauled away. The blue tarp tied over the roof flapped in the salty breeze.

"Are those sandwiches?" Dad asked when he saw the bag in Steven's hand. "I have the best sons in the universe."

Steven handed over the food. "How's it looking?"

Dad sat at the picnic bench near the dock and tore the bag open. "The good news is that the living room and kitchen are okay. The rest of the house, not so much."

"Your room?" Denny asked.

"Wet and soggy."

Steven straddled the bench. "What did Mom say?"

"That we needed a new roof anyway," Dad replied. "And that you shouldn't have any parties on Nathan Carter's boat."

"No parties," Denny agreed.

Dad eyed him. "How's your head?"

"Doesn't hurt," Denny said.

Dad bit into a tuna sandwich and made a happy noise. "I have to wait for the insurance guy from Miami. Why don't you two go relax, I'll catch up to you."

They said they would, mostly to make Dad feel better, but once they were in Steven's truck they decided to go clear out the apartment over the Bookmine. There were only three tiny rooms up there, plus a bathroom that had a tub full of dead palmetto bugs. Layers of dust, stifling heat, and the disturbing smell of rat droppings made Steven pull his T-shirt over his nose.

"I think a hotel is a much better idea," he said.

Denny moved a box and tried to open one of the windows. "You know Mom'll want her own space."

Every room was full of heavy book boxes. It took a dozen trips up and down the rickety staircase to empty the place. They piled the boxes in the far corner of the bookstore's philosophy section, which few people visited anyway. Sean and Robin were too busy at the front desk to offer much help.

"At this rate we'll be done by Christmas," Denny said, once they'd uncovered an ancient sofa and he could plop down on it. Like Steven, he'd sweated through his T-shirt. With the windows open and a fan going the apartment had cooled, though not a lot. "Why don't you call Eddie to come help?"

"You and Eddie don't get along," Steven reminded him. Which was Eddie's fault, really, for being such a homophobic jerk sometimes, but Steven didn't say that.

Denny yawned and tilted his head back. "If he can lift a box, we'll get along just fine."

Steven's phone rang. He knew the caller: Captain Flaherty, over at the Coast Guard station.

"How's your house?" Captain Flaherty asked, loud and cheerful.

"Very well ventilated, sir," Steven said.

Flaherty chuckled. "Nathan Carter called to tell me you're borrowing his boat. I need some transport. Do you think you could come on in to discuss it?"

Steven glanced at Denny. Denny shrugged.

"We'll be there in a half hour," Steven said. After disconnecting he said, "I knew it."

"Knew what?" Denny asked.

"That missing top-secret NASA satellite," Steven said. "The Coast Guard is going to hire us to help find it."

CHAPTER SIX

The Coast Guard station for the Middle Keys was a small collection of concrete buildings and piers that supported five boats. Denny hoped that one day, after he got his commission, he'd be stationed somewhere as busy as this one was with rescues, drug interdiction, and other operations. He really hoped he didn't get posted somewhere freezing cold, like Maine or Alaska. He had no desire to turn into a human Popsicle.

Of course, that all assumed he'd live past age eighteen.

Which, since four o'clock this morning, didn't seem as sure a thing as he'd always taken it to be. Certainly he and Steven had risked their lives on cases. More than once they'd had a too-close call with danger, but honestly? He'd never pictured himself dying because of one rotten oak tree.

The security guard examined Steven's license and let him drive through to the small parking lot. Neither Denny nor Steven had better clothes to change into, but they'd at least washed up and combed their hair.

Most everything was locked up or closed on this Sunday, but a sailor let them into the admin building and escorted them toward Captain Flaherty's office. Steven kept craning his head, probably looking for stray top-secret reports, but nobody had left classified information conveniently exposed. They passed a coffee break room filled with three chatting sailors. A man in a wheelchair was in there, too, punching information into a laptop while scowling at the screen.

"Good to see you both intact!" Captain Flaherty said when they reached his office. He was short and balding, and could pass for a desk jockey except for the triathlon pictures and medals on the wall. "Nice bump."

Denny touched his forehead. He'd pretty much forgotten about it, except when people pointed it out. "Nothing that won't be gone in three weeks, sir."

Captain Flaherty grinned. "Reporting In Day will be here faster than you think. Sit down, sit down."

Steven was barely sitting before he leaned forward eagerly. "How goes the search for that satellite?"

"Satellite? Oh, that NASA equipment. Some kind of weather gauge, I heard. The contractor's out looking for it." The captain ruffled through a sheaf of papers and scanned one. "A company by the name of Othello Industries."

Steven said, "We can help find it."

"I'm sure you could," Captain Flaherty said, lifting his coffee mug. "I had something else in mind, though. My younger brother's gotten himself a new hobby. Underwater photography. Good stuff. That's one of his, over there."

Denny studied the framed twelve-by-fourteen-inch photo on the far wall. The shot had captured another diver suspended in the water between two undersea cliffs. Sunlight filtered down from above, lending light to a dozen shades of blue and green. The picture managed to be completely ordinary but also spectacular at the same time.

"Brad came down to take pictures all week but his charter boat's disappeared," Captain Flaherty said.

Steven asked, "Disappeared?"

Captain Flaherty said, "It was Larry Gold. You know Larry."

Everyone knew Larry. Not the best diver or captain in the Keys, but he could fast-talk the tourists and was generally a nice guy.

His biggest problem was constantly losing money at the Seminole casinos.

Denny said, "There's a dozen dive boats for hire between here and Islamorada."

"Not available for five days on such short notice," Captain Flaherty said. "He's fully certified and has been diving for two years. All you've got to do is take him out and let him follow his bliss. My niece Tristan is with him. She's certified, too, and knows how to help him."

"Help him with what?" Steven asked.

"There's a mobility issue," Captain Flaherty asked. "But again, good money. And I'd consider it a personal favor. Otherwise he's going to be hanging around my house all week, driving my wife crazy."

"I'm the one who owes you a favor, sir," Denny said. "Your recommendation letter helped me get into the academy."

Captain Flaherty shook his head. "You earned that yourself. This is separate. And unofficial, since you don't have a license to run a charter boat. Just say no if you can't do it or aren't comfortable— no hard feelings."

Denny hesitated. He was supposed to be working at the Bookmine, but Mom had already told him to make his own schedule for these last few weeks of his summer vacation. He'd hoped to spend a lot of it with Brian, but if Brian wanted to take things slow, he was going to have a lot of pent-up energy.

"I'm scheduled to lifeguard three days this week," Steven said, "but Robbie Gerstein's been asking for overtime. He could take my shifts."

Denny liked that idea. Working as a lifeguard left Steven too much time to sit around and worry about his SEAL waiver request. A charter would be good for him.

Captain Flaherty picked up a pen. "Here's how much my brother is paying."

He wrote a number on a yellow sticky note and passed it to

Steven. Steven glanced at it and handed it to Denny. Denny's mouth dropped open. He quickly closed it.

Steven grinned. "Tell your brother he's got a charter, sir."

"Tell him yourself," Captain Flaherty said. "He's right down the hall."

❖

"You're kidding," said Brad Flaherty, rolling his wheelchair back a few inches to more fully scowl at Denny and Steven. "You want me to go diving with the Jonas Brothers?"

One of the Coasties in the break room snickered. Steven felt his face heat up. Good money or not, he couldn't see taking this guy out diving without wanting to turn off his tank.

"Dad, please don't use pop culture references you don't understand," said the teenage girl behind him. "Nobody even listens to the Jonas Brothers anymore."

She was short and trim, like a tennis player, and pretty. Really pretty, with long dark hair and hazel green eyes, and the kind of pale skin that said she wore a lot of sunscreen. Not that Steven was noticing much. And he wasn't noticing the way her white shorts clung to her thighs, or the swell of her breasts under her T-shirt, or the glossy shine of her lips.

"They don't look old enough to drive," Brad said.

Captain Flaherty said, calmly, "They can drive, dive, swim, and sail better than most sailors I know, Brad."

Denny said, politely, "We've been diving since we were in middle school, sir. We both have master diver certifications."

Brad's skepticism increased. "You've logged more than fifty dives?"

"You can start when you're twelve years old," Denny said.

Deliberately less polite, Steven added, "We're overachievers."

Brad turned to his brother. "Really, Dermot, this is the best you can do?"

"Daddy, don't be rude," complained the girl. She offered her hand to Steven. "I'm Tristan."

Steven shook her hand. Her fingers were soft, but she didn't have a fancy manicure like many of the girls Steven knew. He said, "I'm Steven, that's Denny. I'm the good-looking one."

She smiled. "You're identical twins."

"Only on the outside," Denny said.

Tristan shook Denny's hand, too. "If you can get my dad on your boat, I can get him down below and out of your hair."

Brad said, "I'm not a piece of cargo."

Tristan kissed his cheek. "But you're being ornery. Don't you think that if Uncle Dermot trusts them, we can, too?"

"I don't trust anyone half my age," Brad groused.

"Except for me," Tristan added.

"And me!" said a kid from the doorway. He was only ten or so, wearing a baggy Coast Guard T-shirt. "I'm like a quarter your age, right, Dad? Look what the chief gave me."

The kid was named Jimmy, and the gift was a small model of a Coast Guard helicopter. Captain Flaherty said, "Jimmy won't be going out to the dives with you—he gets seasick."

"I throw up a lot," Jimmy said emphatically. "Big green chunks. You definitely don't want to see it."

Brad had a mulish expression on his face. "I didn't say I agreed to this. I'm still thinking about the options."

Steven wondered if the man had always been a jerk, or if it was related to whatever had put him into that wheelchair. No one had mentioned Tristan and Jimmy's mother. Maybe there'd been a tragic drunk driving accident that injured him and killed her. Maybe she'd left him after whatever tragedy had paralyzed him. It really was none of his business. Five days of diving, in and out, and he'd have a nice big chunk of money to split with Denny.

Captain Flaherty said, "You're not going to get a better deal, Brad. I trust these boys with my life. Denny's going into the academy in a few weeks and Steven's been accepted for SEAL training."

Steven didn't correct him.

Brad eyed them both top-to-bottom again. Then he rolled back to his laptop and snapped it shut. "Tomorrow morning, eight a.m., where do we meet you?"

"At the city marina," Steven said. "The boat's called the *Idle*."

"Like *American Idol*?" Jimmy asked.

"Not quite," Steven said.

Denny and Steven showed themselves out of the building. They were getting into Steven's truck when Tristan called their names. She caught up to them, a little breathless.

"I wanted to apologize for my dad," she said. "He's just disappointed right now that the other guy didn't show up."

Steven was glad she'd said that. He also liked that some pink had come into her cheeks, the little dimples at the corners of her mouth and the way her shirt fit her. She was about a foot shorter than he was, the perfect size for tucking under his arm and snuggling—

From across the truck hood, Denny said, "We'll take good care of you out there."

Denny slid into the passenger seat. Steven asked, "Do you guys need anything before tomorrow? You've got a place to stay and eat and everything?"

"Oh, sure. We're staying with Uncle Dermot. Aunt Janice makes a mean meat loaf." Tristan squinted up at him. "Also, just so you know, I think you're really cute."

"Yeah?" Steven asked, pleased.

"And I have a boyfriend," Tristan said, folding her arms. "A really big, smart, jealous boyfriend. We're going to Cornell together in the fall. I know you're the kind of guy who's used to getting what he wants, but you're not going to get me."

Steven silently took back every nice thing he had thought about her.

"Well, just so you know, I have a girlfriend," he retorted. "Valedictorian of our class, drop-dead gorgeous, and jealous enough to scratch your eyes out. You look like the kind of girl who thinks she can run the place, but on our boat there's one boss and one boss only."

Tristan lifted her chin. "You or your brother?"

"Both."

"That's two bosses," she said. "I hope you can dive better than you can count."

Steven got into the truck, threw it into reverse, and pulled out of the space with maybe a little more force than necessary.

Denny braced himself against the dashboard.

"What got into your pants?" he asked.

"This is going to be the worst week of my entire life," Steven predicted.

CHAPTER SEVEN

They'd had a very long day but it wasn't over yet. First they stopped to get a new phone for Denny. After that, they went to finish cleaning the apartment. Too late, Denny wished they'd bounced the charter idea against Dad—what if he needed them at the house? When they called him, he said Captain Flaherty had cleared it with him first.

"Besides, unless you both turned into trained roofers overnight, I don't think there's much you can do here," Dad said.

They spent the rest of the day scrubbing down the kitchen, getting the bathroom in reasonable shape, and installing two window air conditioners that had been in storage. By five o'clock they were enjoying cold streams of air, too exhausted to move off the sofa.

"I'm going to fall asleep right here," Denny said, closing his eyes. "Wake me in a week."

Steven grunted. "Can't. Gotta get our scuba gear off your boat and get the *Idle* ready for Sir Brad and Princess Jekyll-and-Hyde."

Someone knocked on the door at the bottom of the stairs. The hinges creaked open. "Denny? You up there?"

Brian's voice. Denny was hot, sweaty, and filthy. It really wasn't the best time to get together. But he said, "Come on up," and sat up, trying to look alert.

Brian climbed the stairs. He had a big flat box in one hand and a grocery bag in the other. "I brought some pizza in case you're hungry."

The pizza smelled deliciously of sausage and cheese and onions. Steven leapt to his feet and snatched it out of Brian's hands.

"You are the most awesome person on this planet right now," Steven said.

"Thanks. And I've got soda and some garlic bread and those cinnamon churro things."

The kitchen table was barely big enough for all the food. Steven inhaled three pieces of pizza with grateful noises that sounded vaguely pornographic. Denny ate more slowly, happy for the food but also nervous. Brian had his serious look on. That had to mean bad news. Maybe his mother was freaking out so much that he'd decided to break up with Denny entirely.

Wouldn't that be the perfect end to a sucky day? First a crashing tree, then a crushed heart.

After another piece of pizza, Steven burped long and loud. "That was the best meal ever. Thanks."

"You're welcome," Brian replied.

For the first time, Steven seemed to notice that Brian and Denny weren't doing much talking. The Bookmine had gone silent beneath them, and the loudest noise was the ancient refrigerator in the kitchen.

Loud knocking interrupted the quiet, followed by a double set of footsteps on the stairs. "Is that pizza I smell?" Sean called out. "I'm famished!"

Robin appeared first in the doorway, carrying a cardboard box. "Thought you might need this stuff up here, so I raided the supply closet downstairs."

Denny took the bag. Toilet paper, paper towels, and more cleaning supplies. Robin had always been the most practical person in their high school class. Sean grabbed for the last churro and said, "Feed us and we're all yours. What do you need done?"

"Nothing," Steven said. "We're finished for the day."

Denny almost argued about that—the bed needed sheets and pillows, half the lamps were missing lightbulbs, and the tub needed scrubbing—but Steven was already scooping up the pizza box and trash.

"I'll meet you back at the marina, Denny," Steven continued, blithely ignoring Sean's disappointment. He headed for the stairs. "Come on, you guys. You can help with the boat."

Sean trailed after him. "I think my mom wants me to babysit…"

Robin also had an excuse. "I'm supposed to take my sister to the movies…"

A moment later, Denny and Brian were alone in the apartment. Brian was perched on the end of his chair, watching Denny with an inscrutable expression. Denny put Robin's supplies on the coffee table and sat on the sofa uneasily.

"Thanks again for the pizza," Denny said. "You didn't have to."

"I tried calling to see what kind you liked, but you didn't pick up."

Denny winced. "Sorry. The new one is still charging."

Brian moved to the battered coffee table in front of Denny and sat on its edges. "This is what I was talking about last night. We barely know each other, right? I don't know if you like pepperoni or anchovies or whatever."

Denny couldn't bear to look at him. Not if they were breaking up. He cut his gaze to the dusty windows and said, "It's not important."

Brian's hands cupped Denny's knees. "It is important. That's why people date. To figure out what they like and what they don't like, what they have in common, what makes that other person interesting. I know that you can swim half an ocean to get help, but I don't know if you like regular Coke or diet."

"Neither," Denny murmured. His hands felt sweaty and his mouth dry. "Are you breaking up with me?"

Brian blanched. "Am I what? No! I want to kiss you. I've wanted to kiss you since I saw you climb out that window this morning."

Relief made Denny almost giddy. "Oh! Well, yeah. You definitely should."

Brian moved next to him on the sofa. Denny turned to him, worried he was going to do it wrong—mash noses, knock Brian's glasses off, put his teeth or tongue in the wrong place. Brian, however, knew what he was doing. He put his hands on Denny's shoulders and his mouth over Denny's and there it was, the heat Denny had been longing for—heat and spark and Brian's firm, confident lips.

"All day long I wanted this," Brian repeated, between kisses. "You are so handsome."

Denny was taller but Brian was heavier, more certain, and lots more experienced. He eased Denny backward against the ratty side cushions and stretched on top of him. Denny was torn between elation—getting kissed, he was getting kissed by a boy, and Brian's hands were stroking his shoulders—and worry that Brian was going to think he was a pushover. But that was silly, right, because Denny just wanted to get as much experience as he could, what did it matter who was on top of whom?

"Relax," Brian urged. "It's just the two of us."

"I know," Denny said.

Brian kissed Denny's jaw, his cheekbone, and his right temple. Each one was like a tiny, pleasurable shock. "I want to find out your favorite movies. Your favorite foods. Your favorite everything."

Denny dug one hand into Brian's back and the other in his blond hair. He pulled him closer. "I'll make you a list."

Brian gave him that sweet, lovely smile that Denny would run a marathon to see. "You can put your hands lower, if you want."

"If I want," Denny repeated, with a giggle, because sure he did. "You don't know how much I want."

Brian kissed him again. And this was even better than before, because Denny was pretty sure he wasn't doing it wrong at all. Confidence made him make a happy noise. He sensed a milestone about to arrive—fantastic, wonderful milestone, no wonder everyone else in high school had been busy having sex while he studied for the Coast Guard Academy—

"Dennis Anderson!" a sharp voice said, completely shattering his elation. "What are you doing?"

Denny bolted upright so fast that he nearly dumped Brian onto the floor. Brian braced himself against the coffee table at the last minute. Denny stared at his aunt Riza, who was standing a few feet away with her suitcase at her feet and her mouth set in a horrified line.

Behind Aunt Riza, Mom finished climbing the stairs and took in the situation.

"Surprise," Mom said. "We came back early. I guess we should have called."

CHAPTER EIGHT

S unset brought pink and gold to the sky, followed by a
twilight that shaded everything to blue-gray. Steven dumped
a bucket of water over the stern of the *Idle* and paused to watch the
bobbing lights of other boats around the marina. He'd retrieved their
diving gear, fueled the tanks, tested the engines, checked the bilge,
and cleaned the galley. He was bone-tired, but also worried that
Nathan Carter's boat wouldn't hold up to the scrutiny of strangers.
Not that he cared what Sir Brad or Princess Tristan thought, but
there was the matter of upholding SEAL pride.

Except Carter wasn't a SEAL anymore, and Steven might never
get to be.

His phone rang. On the other end of the line was Sensei Mike
Kahalepuna, calling from Key West.

"I've got good news for you, kid. Black belt test is this
Saturday."

"This Saturday?" Steven nearly dropped the phone in surprise.
"Talk about short notice."

"You can't do it?"

"Of course we can," Steven said. They'd been asking Mike for
their test since the spring. "We've got a charter that ends Friday and
then we'll drive right down."

"Charter, huh? You're in business for yourself now?"

"Sort of."

"Be sure you get plenty of sleep, drink lots of water, and be at the studio at oh-seven-hundred. The test will take all day. I've got a special surprise, too, and I think you'll be happy about it."

After Steven hung up, he text-messaged the news to Denny's new phone. He'd just pressed Send when he saw Jennifer O'Malley standing on the dock, wearing a white dress and high-heeled shoes.

"Jen," he said, surprised.

"I came to say hi," she said casually. "Heard you had an adventure this morning. You're okay?"

"Yeah, fine," Steven said.

She tilted her head. "Do I have to ask permission to come aboard?"

"No, of course not."

Steven held out his hand and helped her across the short gangplank. She smelled very nice, like lilacs. The scent reminded him of bedsheets and her lace underwear and the last time they'd been together, with sun pouring through the windows and her favorite British singer crooning love songs on the computer.

"Your own yacht," Jen said, standing very close to him on the deck. "I knew you'd have one someday."

"This one's just borrowed." He stepped back an inch or two. "You want something to drink?"

"I'll pass," she replied. "I'm supposed to be on my way to Islamorada to meet Cole for dinner. You remember him?"

"Is he still a jerk?" The last time Steven and Cole had met, Steven had nearly decked the guy. Rich know-it-alls from Miami always rubbed him the wrong way.

Jen smiled faintly. "Don't be jealous. Do you know how much groveling I had to do to get Kelsey to forgive me? She called me every terrible name she could think of, and a few I've never heard before. And I've heard of a lot."

"Sorry," Steven said.

"For sleeping with me?"

"For…" He stopped to think about it. "Well, no. For not being up front with her. I didn't think we were exclusive or anything."

Which was kind of not true, but also not entirely false. Steven didn't like to think too much about it, though. He knew he'd hurt Kelsey and that left him feeling guilty. Everything felt all mixed up, and that was why he was on a vacation from girls. No Kelsey, no Jen, no Melissa Hardy with her double scoops of ice cream at the Dreamette.

"Kelsey's always going to want monogamy," Jen said. "She's hardwired that way. But you and I are different. We believe you should enjoy life while you can, right?"

Somehow her mouth had gotten very close to his. Twilight had given way to night, and a breeze was pushing the hem of her dress against his bare knees.

"Absolutely," Steven said, and then they were kissing.

Which was wrong, all wrong, and totally against his summer vow, but this was Jen. He'd taken off her blouse in eighth grade and her shorts in ninth grade and everything else the Christmas of their junior year. She was clever and sometimes mean and totally not his type—except when she was.

Steven spent a full minute enjoying the taste of cherry lip gloss and the smoothness of her shoulders under his hands. Then he forced out, "Jen, I can't—"

"Show me what's below deck," she whispered.

No normal American teenage boy could possibly resist that, Steven decided. He took her down the short steps into the galley and to the forward cabin. The bed wasn't big or luxurious, but Jen tested it with a grin before reclining on Nathan Carter's beat-up old pillows.

"Come here, sailor," she said.

Steven decided to throw his summer vow out the window.

He had just taken two steps forward when footsteps sounded on the deck above. Quick, forceful steps. Angry.

"Denny?" Steven called out.

His brother stomped down into the galley.

"Just to make it official," Denny announced, "Mom has the lousiest timing in North America."

"What? She's back?" Steven asked.

"With Aunt Riza."

Steven couldn't help but laugh. "She interrupt something important?"

Denny flinched. "I'm glad you think it's funny."

"I don't," Steven said, but of course it was, in a tragic sort of way.

Jen came to Steven's side and adjusted the shoulder of her dress. "Who's the lucky girl, Denny?"

Denny made a sour face, as if he'd sucked on a lemon. "I thought you were on vacation," he said to Steven.

"Vacation from what?" Jen asked.

Steven hoped that Denny didn't answer that. And he got his wish, because Denny immediately turned around and went back on deck.

"Where are you going?" Steven asked.

"To drown myself!" Denny yelled.

A moment later, something splashed into the water.

Steven turned to Jen. "Sorry. Got to go fix my brother."

Jen pouted. "You can't reward him for being a drama queen. Wouldn't you rather stay here with me?"

"Good-bye, Jen," Steven headed up the steps. "Say hi to Cole for me."

By the time he'd kicked off his shoes and peeled off his shirt, Denny was several yards away in the dark water. He was swimming steadily toward the channel markers. Steven could have caught up quickly, but he figured it was better to trail behind. The water was calm and warm, the breeze barely noticeable. Starlight dappled the surface.

Steady strokes, the comfort of the ocean, no place to be.

The world narrowed down to breath and motion, the pleasure of stretching his muscles. Steven almost forgot about Jen and the SEALs as he followed Denny to the markers. For a moment it looked like his twin was going to keep going, out to open ocean, maybe across the sea to Africa or Europe, but Denny stopped to float on his back.

"If I'm lucky, a shark will come along and put me out of my misery," Denny said.

Steven ignored the melodrama and treaded water. "What did Aunt Riza say?"

Denny stared up at the sky. "Nothing good."

"Such as?"

Denny paused for so long that Steven almost repeated the question. Then, reluctantly, he said, "She looked at Brian like he was some kind of sex offender. Then she said I was being foolish and jeopardizing my entire career and why hadn't Mom told her."

Steven could hear Aunt Riza's shrill voice in his head. "How did Brian take it?"

"Better than I did. But not by much. Mom tried to make it better, but you know. When Riza gets going, she gets going. He went home and now he'll probably want nothing to do with this family."

Denny stopped talking. Steven didn't have anything to offer, so he shut up as well. They floated in the ocean, buoyant and quiet, far from the problems of shore. In a few weeks Denny would be gone off to his new life, and Steven left behind with uncertainty, but this moment—well, Steven could hold on to this, and the beauty of the night sky, and the way the ocean tugged him in different directions but also held him aloft.

Eventually Denny started swimming again, and Steven followed. After they climbed back onto the *Idle*, Steven tossed Denny a towel and said, "She's wrong."

"Of course she is." Denny seemed much calmer now, or maybe that was just because he was as exhausted as Steven. "About which part?"

"About being foolish. It'd be more stupid if you had someone who liked you and you just ignored it because you're afraid."

Denny rubbed the towel down his arms and around his feet, which were dripping water on the deck. "It's still illegal in the military."

"You're not in the military yet," Steven reminded him. "Besides, it's not like you're taking him to Reporting In Day and giving him a big smack on the lips in front of the whole student battalion."

Denny cocked his head. "Maybe one day, if the rules change."

Steven snapped his towel at him. "Just ignore Aunt Riza and focus on the next few weeks with Brian."

"When did you turn into Mr. Relationship Advice?"

"About the same time I gave up dating."

"Dating as in bringing girls here and taking off their dresses?" Denny asked. "I don't think that's what Carter had in mind when he said we could use the boat."

"Her dress was still on," Steven protested, but it was a weak excuse. No more women, he vowed once again. And since most of the week was going to be taken up by Tristan and her dad, that would be no problem at all.

CHAPTER NINE

B rian had never been thrown out of anyone else's house before.

Well, to be fair, it wasn't like Mrs. Anderson had shoved him out the door with his pants in his arms. For one thing, his pants had never come off. And Mrs. Anderson had been pretty okay about finding her son getting frisky on the sofa. Denny's aunt Riza, though—well, she was going to be trouble. Brian would be happy never to see her again.

On his way back to the resort he stopped by the Dreamette for a consolatory milkshake. He was surprised to see Sean there.

"Steven tried to put Robin and me to work on his boat, but we lied our way out of it," Sean explained as he paid for a hot fudge sundae.

They sat on one of the picnic benches by the water and Brian explained the sad tale of Aunt Riza.

"Oh, man," Sean said sympathetically. "I've met her. She makes Fidel Castro look like a nice guy. Don't hold her against Denny."

"I won't," Brian promised.

Brian had never hung out with Sean before. He was surprisingly easy to talk to. Unlike a lot of other kids on Fisher Key, he had no grand plan to escape to somewhere bigger and more cosmopolitan. He had enrolled at Key West Community College and never wanted to leave the Florida Keys.

"You never want to see the world?" Brian asked.

"I want to see it," Sean said. "I just don't want to live out there. You can keep the snow, traffic, parallel parking, freeways—"

"Museums, universities, concerts, public transportation—"

Sean slurped hot fudge off his spoon. "You must have hated moving here."

Brian didn't deny it. He'd spend his first few months loathing just about everything about Fisher Key, including the flat landscape and beautiful weather. But then he'd met Denny and started to see the islands through his eyes—the endless beauty of the ocean, the casual lifestyle, the ridiculously romantic sunsets.

"You think you'll ever come back to visit after you go to MIT?" Sean asked.

"I don't know." Brian stirred his milkshake. "I haven't thought that far ahead. I guess it depends on where my mom ends up. And if Denny—well, I don't know. There's always Thanksgiving break and Christmas break. If we're whatever by then."

"You're lucky you found someone around here," Sean said. "And you're both going to be in New England, and what, only a hundred miles apart? If my boyfriend was going to a big fancy college in Boston, I'd spend Christmas making snow angels with him in the middle of the campus. And warming up afterward."

Brian tried to picture Denny in the snow, snug in a winter coat, his nose and cheeks pink from the bitter wind. Denny and *winter* were concepts that did not easily coexist.

"You know him much better than I do," Brian said. "Any tips?"

Sean squinted thoughtfully. "He's not the most transparent guy. I mean, not as transparent as Steven. Do you know that when the *Titanic* hit that iceberg, most of it was underwater? The iceberg, not the *Titanic*."

"Icebergs are usually bigger under the water, yes," Brian agreed.

"Denny's like that iceberg."

"So I shouldn't be the *Titanic*?"

"So you should just, you know." Sean pitched his cup toward the trash bin. "Don't be Kate Winslet."

Brian's phone beeped. It was a message from Mom, making sure he was okay. Which meant she was probably lonely, and drinking. He didn't want to go back to the suite—but he should.

"I don't know what you mean," Brian said. "Kate Winslet's character survived the movie."

Sean replied, "I've never watched the end. It's too sad. You know, just let Denny be Denny. Everything will work out okay."

Back at the suite, Mom was sitting on the sofa in her plush bathrobe. She was drinking white wine and eating celery.

"Did you eat dinner?" Brian asked.

"Sure," she replied. The TV was showing a documentary about whales. "There's some in the refrigerator for you."

Brian poked at a covered plate of ziti and broccoli. He didn't feel especially hungry. When he reached up into the cabinet for a drinking glass, his fingers brushed against a large flat envelope that had been tucked up there.

He pulled it down. His name was on the label and the end had been slit open.

"Mom, what's this?" he asked.

"What's what, honey?"

Brian scanned the letter. His throat tightened up as phrases flew by: *tuition adjustment* and *unexpected shortfall* and *unfortunate circumstances*. When he reached up again he found more envelopes, some from his stepdad's lawyer and others from banks or brokerages.

He took them to his mother and dropped them on the coffee table. They thumped softly.

Brian asked, "When were you going to tell me we're broke?"

CHAPTER TEN

By seven thirty Monday morning Denny was on deck, drinking a very large cup of coffee, his eyelids as gritty as sandpaper. His restless dreams had been full of falling trees and Aunt Riza's frowns and Brian going off to MIT without even saying good-bye. He figured that as tired as he was now, he'd be even more tired during basic training at the academy. At least for now he could relax and enjoy more coffee.

A patrol car parked up near the marina convenience store. Dad came down the dock. He was in full uniform and carrying a bag of groceries along with a doughnut box.

"I thought my children might starve if I didn't bring them nourishment," Dad said as he came aboard.

Denny rescued the box and lifted the lid. He tried not to drool over the chocolate and sprinkles and frosting. "This was Mom's idea, wasn't it?"

"I'll never tell." Dad brushed a touch of sugar from his uniform. "How's your bump?"

"Doesn't hurt at all. How's the house?"

"Roofer's coming out today to do the estimate." Dad sat down on one of the padded benches. "I saw your brother out on the highway. You didn't go running with him?"

"I figured someone should be here if our charter shows up early," Denny said.

"What time's he supposed to?"

"Eight o'clock."

Dad nodded. He poked around in the doughnut box, but didn't take one. Denny broke a plain one in half and dipped it into his coffee, but the serious expression on Dad's face kept him from eating it. Seagulls whirled over their heads, hoping to score a free breakfast.

"Mom wants you to come to the apartment tonight for dinner," Dad said.

One of the gulls landed on the *Idle*'s railing. It only had one foot. Denny always felt bad for one-legged birds. He would have thrown it part of his doughnut, but didn't want to make Dad think he didn't appreciate the gift.

"Aunt Riza's going to make chicken and *maduros*," Dad added.

Denny very carefully did not say where Aunt Riza could put her food.

"I know you're upset with her," Dad said. "But she is your aunt, and she practically raised Mom after they all came from Cuba. Last night maybe went badly—"

"Badly!" Denny said. Talk about an understatement. "Horribly?"

The one-legged gull hopped along the railing, closer to Denny. He said, "I don't want to have dinner with her."

"I know, and I can't blame you," Dad replied. "On the other hand, family's family, and maybe you two can hash this thing out."

"Like the fact she can't stand anybody gay?"

"Did she say that?"

Denny dunked the doughnut again. Little bits of it broke off to sink to the bottom of the cup.

Dad said, patiently, "Denny. Look at me."

Reluctantly he met his father's gaze. One of the hardest things about being a cop's son was that he always expected honesty.

"Not in those exact words," Denny admitted. "But you know that what you look like and your body language say more than words do. That's a principle of human communication."

Dad said, "I'm glad I have a smart kid. So be smart. You know not everyone in the world is going to be delighted that you're gay. They're going to be prejudiced and wrong. That sucks. And it sucks worse when it's your own family. Think of this as an opportunity to show Aunt Riza that being gay doesn't change who you are."

"I shouldn't have to show her," Denny muttered.

"Agreed. But since when is the world fair?"

Steven appeared at the top of the dock, slick with sweat and breathing hard. Denny checked his diving watch. They had fifteen minutes before Brad and Tristan were supposed to arrive. As Steven drew closer he lifted his nose and sniffed appreciatively.

"Are those doughnuts?" he asked. "Yum."

Denny passed him the box. "Eat up. We're having chicken and *maduros* for dinner."

"That's my boy," Dad said.

❖

Steven skipped taking a shower. In an hour or two, he'd be underwater anyway. Instead he hosed himself off, took a bar of soap to his underarms, and then hosed himself again. All done. Their clients were supposed to be on the dock at eight, but the appointed time passed and there was only Denny, Steven, and the diminishing box of doughnuts.

"You want this jelly one?" Steven asked, already reaching for it.

Denny said, "Go ahead. It'll look good on your hips."

"I ran five miles," Steven replied. "My hips can afford two hundred more calories."

Down on the dock, they practiced some blocks and punches in

anticipation of Saturday's black belt test. They also ran through a half dozen katas. The katas, or intricate sequences against imaginary opponents, had to be done precisely and forcefully. Sensei Mike was particularly tough on kata mistakes. He'd been teaching Okinawan Kenpo karate for more than twenty years. The "surprise" that he'd mentioned sounded ominous.

"Maybe he's just trying to psych us out," Steven said, once they'd finished pinon shodan.

Denny reached for a water bottle. "Or he's got something really bad planned."

After the katas, Steven dropped and did fifty of the push-ups required at BUD/S, the SEAL training school. Denny texted someone on his phone—Brian, probably—and Steven turned to sit-ups. Finally, at eight forty, a white van parked in the marina lot and Tristan got out from behind the steering wheel.

Steven was nervous, seeing the wheelchair on the bobbing deck, but Brad navigated with ease. He was fully outfitted in his black wet suit. His mouth was set in a mulish, unhappy line.

"Good morning," Denny said.

"Morning," Tristan echoed, a sunny smile on her face. *Princess Chirpy*, Steven thought to himself. She said, "Sorry we're late."

Her father scowled at Carter's boat. "You're sure she's seaworthy?"

"She's awesome," Steven said. "Come aboard, see for yourself."

It was a little tricky, getting the wheelchair across the gangplank, but they managed. Brad couldn't get down into the galley or up to the wheelhouse, but he studied the contents of the emergency locker and rattled the portable dive platform they'd borrowed from a friend.

"I guess she'll do," he finally said.

Steven asked, "Where's your gear?"

"In the van," Tristan said.

"Let's go get it, then," Steven said, irritated. They'd been hired to take Brad diving, not to be private valets.

In addition to their scuba gear and tanks, Brad and Tristan had brought cases of camera equipment, a cooler full of snacks and sandwiches for themselves, and a book bag with Tristan's initials on it. Steven peeked inside and saw the titles were all about astronomy. So she was some kind of science geek. He knew his constellations but couldn't imagine spending four years studying them.

They'd also brought an extra wheelchair—a rusty, decrepit thing that Steven wouldn't trust to carry a bunny rabbit.

"It's a prop," Tristan said. "For the photo shoots."

It took a half hour to get everything out of the van and stowed on board the *Idle*. It was almost nine thirty before they were ready to set off from Fisher Key. Brad had brought his own charts as well as laminated tables to double-check their dive computers. He'd also printed out pictures from the Internet and drawn up some plans for where he wanted to sink and place the prop wheelchair.

"Here's the list," he said, handing it to Steven. "Everywhere I want to go."

Steven studied it. Some of the sites were easy to get to and easy to dive. Beginner divers liked them a lot. Others were deeper and trickier. The most difficult dive on the list was the *Rumney Marsh*, a research vessel that had been sunk to make an artificial reef.

"We should start with the *Rumney Marsh*," Brad said. "I might want to go back a few times."

Steven passed the paper to Denny and said, "The *Crayford*'s easier, and pretty photogenic."

Brad's gaze narrowed. "You don't think I can do it?"

"I think we'd feel better starting with the easy ones," Steven said, not backing down. "Better that we get to know each other before we tackle the hard ones."

"My brother said you were good," Brad challenged. "He didn't say you were timid."

"Not timid," Steven said. "Cautious. Three years ago someone died diving the *Rumney Marsh*. Two people died last summer, up in Key Largo, similar kind of accident. You want someone to take you there, fine, but it's not going to be us on the first day."

Denny wasn't saying anything. Steven got pissed at that. Usually you could count on Denny to speak up. He was studying the water, his face perfectly blank. The only sounds were the gulls, the chugging of a nearby motor, and the honk of a car horn up in the parking lot.

Tristan broke the stalemate. "I'd rather get to know someone before I dive somewhere dangerous, Dad. Let's do the *Crayford* today. That's on your list, too."

Brad lifted his chin. "Fine. But I'm certified, she's certified, and I expect to get my money's worth once we're all cozy friends."

Denny took the helm and Steven busied himself double-checking his and Denny's equipment on deck. Brad went through his cameras, inspecting cables and batteries. They were twenty minutes out of Fisher Key when Steven spotted three ships south of Bardet Key. One was a Coast Guard cutter and the other two were civilian ships.

"*Othello II*," he said, reading the name on the smaller of the two ships. "They're looking for their lost spy satellite."

Denny shook his head. "You heard Captain Flaherty. It's just a weather monitor."

"He has to say that," Steven said confidently. "He can't go blabbing about national security."

Once the ships were out of sight, Steven went down to the galley to get a bottle of cold water. Tristan was sitting at the table, her feet propped up, reading one of her books. She didn't lift her gaze from the page.

"You don't have to dive with us when we get there," she said. "Dad and I can do fine on our own."

"Part of the service," he replied.

"Because he's crippled and I'm a girl?"

"Because anyone can get into trouble down there," Steven replied. "Decompression sickness, sharks, jellyfish—you name it, we've seen it."

She still didn't look up from her book. "We can handle whatever happens."

"Then I'll be happily bored," Steven said.

When they reached the *Crayford*, two sport fishing boats and a dive boat were already on the site. The dive boat was the *Goat Locker*, run by a retired Navy chief named Darla Stewart. Steven knew she was a good diver, very safe. Stewart must have just arrived because a dozen or so customers were still gearing up on deck. The fishing boats were backing off, per tradition in the Keys, but a dozen other divers were going to make the wreck a little crowded.

"We should have arrived earlier," Brad muttered.

Steven stopped himself from saying something sarcastic.

The sunken ship had an underwater mooring buoy tied to its bow and another to its stern, both designed to keep boaters from dropping anchor on the fragile reef. Denny used the GPS to maneuver to where the stern buoy should be. Steven and Tristan peered over the side to locate it.

"There!" Tristan said, pointing.

Steven took a deep breath, dove into the water, and swam down. The current tugged at him but he had no problem mooring. When he surfaced, Tristan and Brad were slipping on their gear and rigging the wheelchair.

"We'll do two dives here," Brad said. "Then we should head to Thunder Shoals. I want to get some shots in the afternoon light."

Steven said, "Okay, but we should be back at Fisher Key by three o'clock."

Brad's gaze narrowed suspiciously. "We paid you for seven hours per day."

"Which started at eight o'clock this morning," Steven replied.

Tristan put her hand on her father's shoulder. "You know we were late, Dad. Let's just concentrate on the dive, okay? You've been planning this trip for months."

Brad muttered something under his breath and consulted his charts again.

A few minutes later, Steven, Brad, and Tristan splashed over the railing and started their descent, the camera equipment and prop wheelchair with them. Sunlight shimmered around Steven, liquid light illuminating schools of fish darting beneath his flippers. The visibility was excellent, the water seventy-five degrees. Steven grinned behind his mask. He could dive and dive and dive for the rest of his life, each time sparkling new. Too bad Denny had to stay behind on the boat—a dive like this might cheer him up from his funk.

It hadn't been hard to get Brad into the water, and his descent was controlled by his buoyancy compensator vest. He had also brought along a portable propeller or sea scooter to move around without tiring himself. Tristan stayed beside him, her pink bathing suit unmistakable in the blue sea. She filled that bathing suit perfectly, every curve clearly defined, but Steven told his brain not to go there.

The *Crayford* was forty feet down. She was an old cable-laying ship, not much to look at, but years of growth had turned her into a splendid oasis of marine life and plants. They'd only been there a few minutes before divers from Darla Stewart's boat started to appear. Brad set his wheelchair up near the stern and took photographs. Tristan stood watch, waving off other divers if they got in the way. Steven kept an eye on his watch and gauges, but they still had plenty of time.

The other divers swam around them in groups of two and three, snapping their own pictures or underwater video. A girl in a white bikini took Steven's picture and grinned at him from behind her mask. With fifteen minutes left per his watch, Steven signaled Tristan. She nodded. Five minutes later, he gave her the signal to ascend. She tugged on her father's arm, but he brushed her off and held up five fingers. He wanted to push it to their maximum.

Steven didn't like that at all. He swam to Brad and Tristan and once again signaled them to ascend.

Brad shook his head, held up five fingers, and snapped another picture.

Steven wanted to thump the man on the side of his head. Instead, he put his hand over the camera lens. Brad shook him off, angry behind his mask, but Steven insisted with another signal.

Tristan tapped her father on the chest, maybe some kind of symbol between them.

Looking annoyed, Brad started upward.

They stopped at fifteen feet for a three-minute safety stop. But Brad broke upward at least thirty seconds early, which pissed Steven off even more. He waited, though, unwilling to risk the bends. By the time he surfaced, Brad was clinging to the dive platform and berating Denny.

"—don't need a babysitter, and I'm not some kind of idiot newbie who doesn't know the risks—"

Denny, to his credit, was giving Brad his best blank face. He said, "Why don't we get you back on board and we'll settle it then?"

"Not a newcomer," Brad repeated, hauling himself up on the platform as far as he could. "Crippled doesn't mean stupid."

Tristan, bobbing in the water beside Steven, said, "Dad, you knew time was up."

Steven shrugged off his tank and flippers, swung them up to Denny, and hauled himself up the platform ladder. Together, he and Denny lifted Brad back into the boat. Steven tried not to stare at the man's long, useless legs and focused instead on what a jerk he was being.

"So what exactly happened down there?" Denny asked, handing out towels.

"He ignored the timetable," Steven said.

"I knew exactly how much time I could spend," Brad retorted.

"Dad, you didn't—" Tristan started.

"I don't need your input, Tris," her father snapped.

Denny jerked his head toward the galley and Steven followed him. Once below, away from where they could be overheard, Denny turned on Steven angrily.

"Are you trying to ruin my career, or what?" he demanded.

CHAPTER ELEVEN

W hy are you mad at me?" Steven snapped. "I'm not the one putting myself in danger."

"If he gives a bad report about us to Captain Flaherty, word will get around," Denny said hotly. "I don't need a bad reputation before I even show up at the academy."

Steven rolled his eyes. "You'd rather be known for cutting corners and letting people walk all over you?"

"I'm not letting—"

"You're being an asshat," Steven said. "Safety first, all the time. That's the rule."

Denny folded his arms. "I think this is personal. He rubs you the wrong way and you keep snapping at him. Two alpha dogs barking and barking."

"Alpha dog?" Steven asked scornfully. "That's what you think?"

"I think you better lay off before you ruin this," Denny said.

Steven said, "Fine. You deal with him. I'll take the wheel and shut up for the rest of the day."

Steven stomped his way up to the wheelhouse. After the mandatory rest period, Brad and Tristan descended again with Denny at their side. Steven brooded and glowered across the waves at Darla Stewart's boat, where a group of divers were also readying for their second descent. The breeze had picked up and some rain clouds were gathering in the west, but the forecast remained mostly okay.

He had nothing to do but wait, wait and wait some more. Because of nitrogen buildup, Tristan and Brad couldn't dive as long on this trip. Steven hoped, pettily, that salt water got into Brad's camera and ruined it. But when the trio surfaced a short time later, Brad seemed in a good mood and Tristan was grinning.

"We saw a huge grouper," she said. "At least six hundred pounds!"

"Seven hundred," Brad said, handing his camera gear up.

Denny slipped off his tank. "The locals call him Fred. He's a celebrity."

They got Brad settled back on the boat, as well as the prop wheelchair and other equipment. Denny let them loose from the underwater buoy and Steven steered them toward Thunder Shoals, a shallow section of the reef where they could snorkel freely. Steven didn't say anything to Brad or Tristan and responded minimally to Denny. It occurred to him that maybe he was being childish, but so what? It felt good to sulk.

Tristan climbed up to the wheelhouse on the way to Thunder Shoals. She had pulled on a long-sleeved jersey and had a book tucked under her armpit.

"Can I steer?" she asked.

"Do you have a boater's license?"

"No."

"Then no. You can steer when you have a license," he said primly.

Tristan scowled. "You like rules, don't you? Is that why you want to go into the military?"

"It's not about rules," Steven said. "It's about not getting killed and not doing stupid stuff."

"My dad knows what he's doing."

"A lot of people who know what they're doing still do stupid things." Through the window, Steven watched a flock of seagulls swirl against the sky. "Like pushing the table or skipping safety stops."

Tristan asked, "And you've never done either one?"

"Never."

She made a little noise of disbelief.

"You think I want to permanently damage myself? Brain damage or lifelong pain or paralysis?" A sudden thought occurred to him. "That's how it happened, isn't it? That's why he's in a wheelchair now."

"Don't be stupid," she said. "He was injured in Iraq, six years ago."

Steven asked, "He was a soldier?"

Tristan stared out at the sea. "No. A civilian journalist embedded with the U.S. Army. A suicide bomber hit the mess hall in the middle of dinner."

"I'm sorry to hear it," Steven said, truthfully.

"If he's temperamental, it's because he's had to fight every day for the last six years," she said. "For good medical care, for permanent disability benefits, for everything. There've been lawyers and lawsuits and more lawsuits, and do you know how many journalist jobs there are these days? He had to completely change careers."

"What does he do now?"

"Teaches at a community college," she said. "And hates it, but that's all there is. Two years ago one of his counselors set him up with scuba diving to relieve stress and depression. He and my mom got certified together."

Steven asked, "So where's she?"

"She left him," Tristan said. "Anything else you think you need to know about my family?"

"No," Steven said. "I just need to know that he won't do anything stupid or dangerous down there."

"Trust me," she said. "We're not suicidal."

❖

Three other boats were moored to the floating buoys at Thunder Shoals. The reef was only fifteen feet down, covered with several varieties of beautiful, brilliantly colored coral, with fish swarms and occasional nurse sharks. Brad, Tristan, and Denny went into the water with snorkel gear, leaving Steven on board to mind the helm. Denny noticed that Tristan had gone up to talk to him and afterward, Steven had seemed in a more thoughtful mood. Maybe things would get better between him and their clients.

After the snorkeling, Steven turned back to Fisher Key. Denny helped Brad and Tristan rinse the seawater from their equipment. Brad seemed satisfied with the afternoon's results.

"Tomorrow we should head out to Sombrero Reef," he said.

Denny breathed a silent sigh of relief that there would be a tomorrow—that they weren't fired. He was still stinging from Steven's accusation that he was being a doormat. Compromising and listening to both sides of a story didn't mean he was a pushover. But he didn't want Captain Flaherty hearing complaints about Steven being unprofessional.

Then again, Brad might be the kind of person to complain no matter how much you tried to please him.

Denny joined Steven in the wheelhouse for the final leg of the trip back to Fisher Key. Steven said, "You want the wheel?" which, for him, was sort of an apology.

"No, you keep it," Denny replied. And then, because he accepted the apology, he added, "As long as you don't ram us into the dock."

"Tristan said her dad got hurt as a civilian in Iraq," Steven said. "Sucks, huh?"

"Recently?"

"About six years ago."

"We were only in sixth grade," Denny mused.

"Doesn't excuse him for being dangerous," Steven said.

"I know." Denny didn't say anything else. Sometimes it was best to let Steven stew over his ideas and figure them out on his own.

As they turned into the marina, Denny saw that the civilian ship *Othello II* had moored at the outermost pier. Up close, she was about fifty feet long with a large A-frame and winch on deck. He was surprised they were in port so early in the afternoon. Steven said, "They must have found what they were looking for."

"Or they had mechanical problems," Denny said.

Steven docked the *Idle*. Denny went down to make sure Brad got to the pier safely. Steven helped as well, and if he wasn't very talkative to Brad at least they didn't snap at one another. The twins helped Tristan carry the cameras and other equipment back to their van.

"We'll be back tomorrow at eight," Brad said. And then, maybe as his own sort of apology, he said, "Promptly at eight."

"We'll see you then," Denny said.

Steven only nodded.

On their way back to the *Idle*, Denny made a list in his head of everything they had to do, including refuel the boat, check the weather forecast, check the dive tanks, make sure everything was rinsed off and stowed properly. And, oh yes, have dinner with homophobic Aunt Riza. He'd tried not to think about it too much, preferring to concentrate on the ocean and diving, but his stomach clenched in anticipation of a tense and unhappy dinner.

As they passed the *Othello II*, a pretty blond woman inspecting some scuba tanks leaned over the railing and smiled at them. "Hi there! Are you locals?"

"As local as you can get," Steven said.

"I was looking for the nearest grocery store." She swung down to the deck, tanned and fit in khaki shorts and a yellow polo shirt. "I'm Claire. Claire Donovan."

"The marina store has groceries," Denny said.

"I'm looking for some tofu," Claire said, and how her accent came through—Irish, Denny thought. She said, "I'm vegetarian. The marina store's more of a carnivore kind of place."

"There's a health store on U.S. 1, about three miles north," Steven said, returning her smile. Denny watched in amazement. He swore that half the time Steven didn't even know he was flirting. It was some kind of default setting, hardwired into him.

"Can I bike there?" Claire asked.

"There's no bike lane," Steven said. "I'm going to the dive shop up there, if you want a ride."

This was news to Denny. They'd agreed he would borrow Steven's truck and fill the tanks. On the other hand, if Steven wanted to make a fool of himself with an older woman, Denny could stay behind and maybe get some time with Brian before the dinner with his family.

Claire said, "I don't want to impose."

"No imposition," Steven said.

As soon as they were gone, Denny messaged Brian. Brian arrived twenty minutes later, his clothes and face creased as if he'd been sleeping.

"You okay?" Denny asked.

Brian stepped up on the *Idle*. "Long night."

Denny grimaced. "Was it my aunt? I know she was rude. I'm so sorry—"

"No, it's not your aunt," Brian said. "It's just my mom. And the lawyers, and the accountants, and the financial people at MIT."

"What about them?" Denny asked, alarmed.

Brian sat and ran a hand through his tousled hair. "It turns out that my stepdad didn't have as much money as he said he had, and what's left is getting snatched up by his lawyers. Mom's been hiding the letters from me while she tries to work it out, but I don't know. I need twenty thousand dollars."

Denny sat beside him on the deck. "They can give you loans, right?"

"Maybe. But we didn't qualify for financial aid, so we didn't fill out any forms, and now it might be too late…it's all a mess." Brian leaned forward, elbows on his knees, and made a visible effort to calm down. "How was your day?"

Denny leaned back. "Well, the diving was good. Steven was kind of cranky. It would have been more fun if you'd been along."

"Maybe tomorrow," Brian said, sounding not very interested. Then he lifted his head. "Actually, yeah, maybe tomorrow. It'd be nice to have a break from Mom."

Technically, Denny needed to ask for Brad's okay. He might not want another person on the boat he was paying for. But a worse possibility, and one that Denny really should have thought of before he brought it up, was Brad or Tristan might figure out Brian and Denny were more than just friends.

"We couldn't…" Denny waved his hand. "You know. Be affectionate."

"Why not?" Brian asked.

"Because this guy might tell his brother. His brother who's the Coast Guard captain."

"Denny…" Brian started, but then he stood up. "Never mind. I've got to get going."

"No, wait! Don't you want to…you know. Hang out for a while?" Denny didn't mention there was a bed below deck and they'd be alone for at least an hour before Steven came back. He didn't remind Brian there were exactly twenty-one days remaining before he had to report to New London. He just wanted Brian to stay and hang out.

"Face it, you're embarrassed to be seen with me," Brian replied.

"What? No! I'm not embarrassed," Denny insisted. "You know what the situation is like. It's about being discreet."

Brian took off his glasses and cleaned them with his shirt. "I know you want to keep things low. And I thought I could do okay with that. But this week—I need someone to lean on in public. You want someone to hide in public."

Denny corrected him. "What I want is a career in the military."

Brian slid his glasses back on. "And I want to go to MIT, and for my mom to stop crying herself to sleep, and for a boyfriend who's not afraid to hold my hand in front of other people. We just can't always get what we want, right?"

Pressure squeezed against Denny's lungs as if he was diving too deeply into the ocean. "Are you breaking up with me?"

"No," Brian said. "Maybe. I don't know. Call me later and we'll figure it out."

He walked away, up the dock, away from Denny. The sun was behind him, so bright it made Denny's eyes water. He looked away and dragged his sleeve across his face. Stupid, stupid sunlight.

CHAPTER TWELVE

Claire Donovan came from the village of Glendalough in County Wicklow, Ireland. Steven said he didn't know where County Wicklow was, but he bet the scuba diving wasn't as good as it was in Fisher Key.

"There's plenty of diving," Claire said, full of mock indignation. "Caves and reefs, bays, coves, some very lovely wrecks. You'd be surprised."

Steven stopped for a red light. "But it's not as warm."

She smiled. "Not as warm, I grant you that."

"Is that what you do?" he asked. "Commercial scuba diving?"

Claire studied the shops on the side of the road—bait and tackle, souvenirs, and the Gas'n'Go. "Oceanographer," she said, and it sounded deliberately vague to him. Because when you had a top-secret job, you had to use deflection.

The light changed to green and Steven accelerated. Traffic was moderate at this time of day, with tourists coming back from their charters and people passing through on their way to other places. He asked, "You're out there looking for that lost weather satellite, aren't you?"

Claire's phone buzzed in her pocket. She pulled it out, scanned the message, and typed something on the tiny keyboard. Her fingernails were short and unpolished. "How did you hear about that?"

"Word gets around," Steven said. "It's not every day that a rocket misfires."

"A very expensive and valuable rocket with a very expensive and valuable payload," she replied, putting the phone away. "Hopefully we'll find it in a day or two and get back home to Norfolk. What is it you do? Still in school?"

"Oh, no, I graduated," he said, neglecting to mention it had only been a few weeks ago. "Working for the summer on a friend's boat."

"And then?"

"I've got some options I'm thinking over." Steven spied the turn-in for Natural Ann's, the health food store, and slowed down. "Here we are. I can top off these tanks and come back to give you a ride."

"I don't want to be a bother," Claire said.

He dropped her off at the front door. "No bother at all."

As he drove to the dive shop he told himself it wasn't as if he was asking her on a date, or trying to spark something between them—sure, she was pretty, and he liked her smile, but his interest was professional only. And when he picked her up and took her back to the marina, it was totally professional as well—he asked about her company, and what they did up in Norfolk, and what kind of jobs they had there. Claire said her department studied ocean currents and that she was employed as a doctoral student. She had to submit and defend her thesis in the fall.

"Then you'll be Dr. Claire?" Steven asked.

"If all goes well."

Back at the marina, he carried a grocery bag for her down to the *Othello II*. A man in khaki pants and a white shirt was on deck. He wasn't much older than Claire, maybe twenty-five or so years old, and he struck Steven as one of those rich kids like Jen's friend Cole—good-looking, silver spoon, think they owned the world.

"Jamie Harrison," he said, introducing himself. "I'm the ship's diver. Thanks for giving Claire a lift."

"Anything for a neighbor," Steven said, not flinching at all under the man's extra-firm handshake. "I'm Steven."

"You live around here with your folks?" Harrison asked.

Steven understood that was a subtle dig. Or not-so-subtle. He nodded toward the *Idle.* "I'm living aboard there."

Harrison's gaze flickered to Carter's old fishing boat, with its peeling paint. He looked a little skeptical, or maybe that was amusement. Like he thought Steven was a kid playing grown-up.

"How's the engine, Jamie?" Claire asked.

"Not so good," Harrison replied. "Looks like we're stuck in port for the night. Maybe there's some place around here to kill time."

Claire climbed up on deck. Steven passed up the grocery sack and said, "There's some bars if you're in the mood for Jimmy Buffet and pink margaritas."

Harrison grinned. "Not my style."

"Your style is to obsess over charts all night," Claire said cheerfully. "The girl at the store said the yacht club has a restaurant and lounge."

"Kind of quiet there," Steven said. And, worse, the bartenders had a bad habit of chasing him out because they all knew he was underage and definitely knew his dad.

"I'm sure we'll find something," Claire said. "Thanks again, and maybe we'll see you later."

"Okay," Steven replied.

Harrison grinned, a glint in his eyes, and Steven figured the man thought he had a crush on Claire. Which was totally not true.

Still, as Claire went below deck, Steven had to force himself not to stare at her receding profile. Strictly professional, he told himself.

Plus, she was older. A lot older, like six or seven years. A woman with a professional degree and a good job.

And he was eighteen years old, no job in sight, no word from the SEALS, on his way to what was not going to be the happiest of dinners with his family.

"See you around, kid," Harrison said, climbing back aboard his boat.

Steven walked back to the *Idle* and pulled out his phone. Sometimes you had to go it alone, and sometimes you needed reinforcements.

"Hi," he said after dialing. "What are you doing later?"

CHAPTER THIRTEEN

Y ou go first," Denny said, dread filling his gut.

"Don't be a wimp." Steven swung open the door to the Bookmine's upstairs apartment. He took the stairs two at a time and called out, "Mom! We're home!"

The apartment would never be home, but it definitely looked better than they had left it. The unfinished floor had been covered with blue area rugs, the sofa was wrapped with a blue and green slipcover, and vintage posters of Cuba had been moved upstairs from Mom's office. Potted plants dotted the windowsills and the whole place smelled like chicken and plantains. Denny's stomach growled despite his nerves. He stood back while Aunt Riza gave Steven a big hug and kiss.

"Look how tall you both are," Aunt Riza said, fawning over Steven. "My handsome nephews. Denny, come here, give me a kiss."

He submitted as gracefully as possible, trying not to wrinkle his nose at her heavy perfume. "The place looks great," he said.

"You two did most of the work," Mom said from the counter, where she was tossing a salad. Neither of Denny's parents was adept in the kitchen, but under close supervision you could trust them with small vegetables, frozen dinners, and soup from a can. "We just added the womanly touches."

"And manly ones, too," Dad said, trudging out from the small bathroom. He rubbed a towel against his wet head. "How was your day at sea?"

"It was great," Steven said cheerfully. "No problems."

Denny was trying to check his phone without being too obvious about it. He'd called Brian on the ride over, but there was no answer. He added, "And we met the contractors looking for that weather satellite."

"They haven't found that yet?" Dad asked.

"What satellite?" Mom asked.

They told her about Steven's shooting star and the NASA satellite. Aunt Riza bustled around, busy with the frying *maduros*. Denny volunteered to set the table but as soon as he did, he worried Aunt Riza would see it as a girly thing, a gay thing, and he got mad at himself. He'd set the table at home a hundred times.

Just to be safe he said, "Steven, get the glasses."

Steven let himself be drafted into helping. Dad sat on the sofa and asked them more about Brad Flaherty. Steven volunteered he'd been paralyzed in Iraq.

"Poor man." Aunt Riza wiped her hands delicately on a dish towel. She was probably the only person in Fisher Key making dinner while wearing a dress and high heels, but that was Riza for you—always properly dressed, never barefoot. She continued, "And scuba diving! So dangerous. How does he kick down if he can't use his legs?"

"You don't descend underwater by kicking your feet," Denny said. "That's what the vest is for."

Aunt Riza had never been scuba diving—neither had Mom. Dad was the one who'd gotten the boys interested, back before they started high school, but he hadn't done much of it lately. Denny didn't understand why someone would give up all that beauty and the challenge of going places few other people got to go. Dad explained to Aunt Riza how the BC vest was inflated or deflated and thus controlled ascent or descent. By the time he was done with the details, they were sitting at the table and digging into a mountain of food that could probably feed a restaurant full of customers.

"Tastes great, as always," Dad said.

To Denny, the chicken tasted bland and the plantains burnt. Not that he could say anything. He picked at the food, darting glances every now and then at Mom. She was trying to look pleasant, but her expression was strained. Riza was the sister who had cared for her, raised her and loaned her the money to buy the Bookmine. Her approval was really important to Mom.

But so was Denny's happiness, right?

The clock in the kitchen ticked quietly. The only sounds were the scrapes of forks on the dinner plates. Denny's phone did not vibrate with any message from Brian asking him to come over. Steven darted his gaze from his parents to Denny to his aunt, and too late Denny recognized the look on his brother's face.

"So," Steven said, "what about the gay thing?"

Denny kicked him. Dad coughed.

Aunt Riza's expression remained unruffled behind her pink-rimmed eyeglasses. "There's no such thing. I didn't see what I thought I saw."

Denny's face grew hot. "Sure you did."

"Denny," Dad warned.

"She did!" Denny insisted. "She saw it and I'm not embarrassed about it."

"There's nothing to be embarrassed about," Mom said, patting Denny's arm.

Blithely Steven said, "I'd be embarrassed if Mom caught me making out with Kelsey. Some things you just don't want to share with your closest relatives."

"And I think that pretty much sums up the matter," Dad said, obviously hoping that they'd move on from the topic.

Denny's fingers had gone numb from gripping his fork too tightly. "It doesn't! If anyone caught Steven—and believe me, it's not hard, he makes out with every girl on this island—you'd all just laugh it off. But I kiss a boy and it's a national emergency."

Steven protested, "I don't make out with every girl on this island."

Dad muttered, "Seems like it."

Aunt Riza sliced into her chicken with sharp strokes of her knife. "Of course it's not an emergency. But soon you'll be away, the first ever in our family to go to the Coast Guard Academy, and you'll meet some nice smart girls."

Before Denny could answer *that*, Mom swiftly said, "And to celebrate your going away, Riza's going to have a pool party at her house. All your cousins will be there, and your aunts and uncles, and there's going to be a big feast of food."

"For you and your brother both," Aunt Riza said. "For when he gets his waiver on this silly eye test that's causing so much trouble."

Steven flushed. Denny was glad to see him squirm. Lying about being admitted to BUD/S had been one of the stupidest things Steven had ever done, and their parents hadn't been pleased.

"I could do a party," Steven said casually. "When?"

"Saturday," Mom said. "In Miami."

Denny really couldn't feel his fingers anymore. He dropped the fork and flexed them, hoping he hadn't given himself permanent nerve damage. "We can't!"

Simultaneously Steven said, "We have our black belt test Saturday."

"I told you," Denny said to his father.

"Did you?" Dad asked, surprised.

Denny was sure that he had, but now he couldn't specifically remember. "I thought I did. This morning, when you brought the doughnuts."

Steven said, "It's an all day thing. We're going down Friday night, just to make sure we're not late."

"They can reschedule the test," Aunt Riza said confidently. "All of your family is coming, and I can't change the invitation."

Denny said, "You could have asked."

Mom looked desperately unhappy. "Denny. Please."

He felt bad for her, he really did, but still he said, "You can't just call up your sensei and tell him to move the test."

Aunt Riza remained unfazed. "I'll call him. Surely he'll understand."

"Maybe you could even invite him," Dad suggested.

Steven stopped eating. Which was so rare for him that it usually meant a medical or emotional emergency. "Dad, you're not helping."

"Maybe he could postpone it if you explain it," Mom suggested. "Or you could take it on Christmas break."

The table fell silent. The only person eating was Aunt Riza, who had devoured her chicken all the way to the bone.

"Well," Dad finally said, "how about some dessert?"

"I'm not hungry," Denny said.

"Neither am I," Steven added.

Aunt Riza said, "But I made flan. Your favorite!"

Denny almost told her where she could take her flan and stick it. But one look from his father quelled the impulse right away, so he kept his mouth shut and ate the damn custard.

CHAPTER FOURTEEN

Eddie was home, just as he'd promised he'd be. The house didn't look much cleaner than the last time Steven had come over. In fact, it looked worse than the last time Steven had come over—dirty clothes piled in the living room, stale pizza boxes stacked on the kitchen counter, and garbage overflowing out of the kitchen trash can. It could have won an award for "Stinkiest House on Fisher Key," but Steven didn't think Eddie would appreciate the honor.

"What's wrong with you?" Eddie asked. "You look pissed off."

"One awesomely awkward dinner for five, done with." Steven flopped down on the sofa and ignored the jab of a broken spring against his hip. "I hope I never have to go through that again."

Eddie leaned back in an ancient, threadworn recliner. "Why so awkward?"

"Long story." Steven didn't think Denny would appreciate if he shared all the gritty details. "Anyway, what's new here?"

"Still unemployed, still no chance of going to college, and I broke up with Lisa," Eddie said.

"You did? Why?" Not that Steven liked Lisa. He thought she was pretty skanky sometimes. But for the sake of guy solidarity, he ought to at least look sympathetic.

"Because she's been seeing Carl Trost."

Steven frowned. "Isn't he like twenty-four years old?"

"Yeah," Eddie said. "But he has a job."

"Tending bar."

Eddie shrugged. "Good tips."

Steven and Eddie watched a movie for a while, some old comedy that hadn't been very funny the first time. Eddie kept checking his phones and trading text messages with someone. Steven pictured himself sitting on the same lumpy sofa five years into the future, ten years maybe, and neither of their lives would have changed. They'd grow beer bellies and lose their hair and these cushions that smelled like bad milk would just smell even worse.

"You've got that look on your face," Eddie said.

"What look?"

"Like you're trying to swallow a rock."

Steven shrugged. "Nothing. I don't know. We're supposed to take the black belt test on Saturday."

"Yeah? That's a good thing, right?"

"It's okay." Steven didn't want to go into the whole Aunt Riza affair. Nothing had been resolved about that. She hadn't changed her plans and Mom and Dad wanted them to reschedule the test. Telling Sensei Mike they couldn't make it was about the last thing that Denny or Steven wanted to do.

Plus, the family celebration in Miami sounded like a bad idea all around. Steven liked his relatives, but everyone was going to ask about BUD/S and SEAL training and when he was going away. He would either have to lie a little, lie a lot, or admit the truth.

He should *never* have lied about being accepted.

Steven wondered if Denny would agree to go to the celebration—it was for him, after all—and let Steven go to Key West by himself.

No, that would suck. They'd come this far together in their training and he wanted them to get their black belts together, too.

When Eddie went to the bathroom, Steven took his phone outside and called Sensei Mike. The call went to voice mail, but he didn't leave a message. He called Sensei Teresa instead. She was Mike's right-hand assistant when she wasn't running a fleet of trolleys carrying tourists around the island all day long.

"I'm so excited about your test on Saturday!" she said, over the thumping of music and voices in some bar. "You're going to be awesome."

"I hope," Steven said. "Do you know if—"

Teresa interrupted him. "And the surprise! I haven't seen him this excited for a test in years."

Denny had mentioned something about that. Steven asked, "What kind of surprise is it?"

"I can't tell. Sworn to secrecy."

"Just one hint. Animal, rock, mineral?"

She laughed. "None of the above. Stop pestering me and go practice your katas. And your kicks! Kicks and katas, kiddo. You're going to do about a hundred thousand of them this weekend."

Steven hung up. He tilted his head up to the stars and tried to figure out exactly what kind of surprise Sensei Mike had in mind. Maybe he'd arranged to hold it somewhere other than the dojo, which was an old coffee mill. Or maybe he'd built in some extra-special challenge, like breaking planks. He worried that if they tried to reschedule the test it would be some kind of mortal insult, and they'd disappoint Sensei Mike forever.

Or they could disappoint Mom and Dad and Aunt Riza, all because Aunt Riza hadn't even bothered to ask them if they were free on Saturday.

Eddie yelled through the open screen door, "You coming back in? You're letting out all the air-conditioning."

Which was a joke. Eddie's mom had a couple of different jobs, but Eddie was unemployed. They didn't have enough money to run an air conditioner except on really hot days.

"I'm coming," Steven said, and went back to sit on the lumpy and sour-smelling sofa.

Chapter Fifteen

When he and Steven had left the Bookmine apartment, Denny had been tempted to go right over to the resort. He wanted to tell Brian about how awful dinner had been, and Aunt Riza's refusal to move the party on Saturday, and how Denny's parents had been totally unhelpful.

On second thought, however, none of that would cheer Brian up. He had his own significant problems to deal with. And they were maybe broken up, or maybe not, and Denny wasn't sure that Brian even wanted to see him.

The idea that Brian didn't like him anymore made Denny feel like another tremendous tree had come crashing down, and this one was suffocating him. No fire department could lift this weight. You couldn't chain-saw someone into forgiving you.

Steven had been headed for Eddie's house. He dropped Denny back at the marina. As Denny walked down the dock he saw lights and heard music from the yacht club on shore. A handful of people were sitting on the deck of the *Othello II*, watching a baseball game on a portable television.

"Hi, Steven," Claire called out. "Red Sox or Rays?"

Denny replied, "Rays. And I'm the other one. Denny."

"There's two of you?" asked the cute guy nearest the TV.

"You're the one going to the Coast Guard Academy," Claire said. "I heard that up at the store."

"Swab summer!" the cute guy said. "Good luck to you."

Denny wanted to go back to the *Idle* and mope, but it turned out that the cute guy—Jamie Harrison—had been stationed in the Navy in Groton, Connecticut, just across the river from the academy. He'd dated a cadet for a while. Harrison didn't really look old enough to be prior military, but he'd served for four years right out of high school and then decided not to reenlist.

"Got tired of the uniforms," Harrison said, after Denny had come aboard and taken a seat. "And the officers. No offense, but what a bunch of stuck-up idiots."

Denny said, dryly, "I'll try not to become one of those."

Claire either didn't know or didn't care that he was underage. She handed him a nice cold beer from the cooler. Denny was happy to have it. The other person on deck with them was another diver named Bud. Bud was older than Claire and Jamie both, with wire-rimmed glasses and a Red Sox baseball cap.

"I can't believe anyone likes the Rays," Bud said.

"Home state," Denny reminded him.

Harrison said, "Bud doesn't believe there's intelligent life below the Mason-Dixon Line."

Bud replied, "Not true. I said there were no good baseball teams below the Mason-Dixon Line."

Denny felt obliged to defend the Marlins, Rays, and Braves. It helped that Tampa Bay was currently beating the pants off the Red Sox. Sitting under the stars as the boat rocked gently, drinking beer and talking baseball, Denny could almost forget the problems with Brian, Aunt Riza, and the black belt test. He liked Harrison, who was frank and forthright and obviously more than a little interested in Claire, who pretended to know nothing about the game. She kept asking Bud when the touchdowns would be coming or who the quarterback was.

"You kill me, Irish Springs," Bud said, and dug more beer out of the cooler.

During a commercial Claire said, "Denny, if you're going away in three weeks, why aren't you spending tonight with a special girl? Time's short."

"It's not like you're going to have time to date for the next few months," Harrison put in. "My friend never had a moment to herself as a swab, and it didn't get much better her first year."

"It's okay," Denny said. "We're...on a break, I think. Kind of."

Claire's face lit up. Her gaze was slightly unfocused from the alcohol. "Did you cheat on her?"

"No," Denny swore.

"Forget her birthday?" Bud asked.

"No."

Harrison asked, "Didn't make her feel special enough? Because sometimes we forget to tell them."

He was gazing at Claire as he said it. She ducked her gaze and smiled.

Denny said, "Maybe that's it."

"Take her somewhere special," Bud said. "Nice romantic evening and a nice hotel room. What are we, an hour from Key West?"

Denny kept his eyes on the game. But inwardly he thought, *Yeah, Key West*, and if there was ever a place to be public and private at the same time, it had to be at one of the resorts that catered to gay tourists. He should have thought of it earlier.

But Brian might not want to leave his mom, not with everything going on right now.

Denny sighed and drank some more beer. He barely had the energy to celebrate when Tampa Bay won. Bud was still moaning over it when Steven returned from Eddie's house. Steven seemed surprised to see Denny sitting on the deck of the *Othello II*.

"Hello, Steven!" Claire said. "You missed the game!"

"Terrible game," Bud added.

Denny said, "Because Florida won."

"Of course Florida won," Steven said.

Harrison snapped off the TV. "So there really are two of you. Are you going to the Coast Guard Academy like your brother?"

"Not at all," Steven said. "Come on, Denny. We've got to be up early."

"I know," Denny said, annoyed, because he wasn't a little kid who needed a reminder. When he stepped down to the dock, it swayed a lot more than usual. Only then did he think that maybe he'd had more to drink than he'd intended. Steven caught his arm and muttered something unflattering.

"Good night, boys," Claire said, amused, as Harrison slung his arm around her shoulder and looked down at them.

Harrison added, "Have a safe trip home."

"Game two of the series is tomorrow night!" Bud yelled. "Go Red Sox!"

The walk back to the *Idle* would have been easier if the horizon wasn't moving so much. The smell of seaweed and old fish made Denny's stomach lurch.

"Why'd you hang out with those guys?" Steven asked. "You don't even know them."

"They're okay," Denny said. "Nice."

The dock slid sideways. Steven grabbed Denny's arm. "Harrison's a jerk. And you turned into a lightweight when I wasn't looking."

"Not a lightweight. It's just been a long, long day," Denny said.

Back on Carter's boat, Steven dumped Denny into the bed and went to make up the galley berth for himself. Denny watched the overhead spin and tried to remember the name of that resort he'd seen during his last trip to Key West. He and Brian could have a romantic weekend together. If Brian still liked him. If Denny hadn't ruined everything.

He found his phone and sent a long heartfelt message.

Steven came back with a glass of water and some aspirin. "Take these."

Denny hated the taste of the pills, but he swallowed them anyway. "Why don't you like Harrison? He's cute."

"He's not cute to me," Steven replied.

"What are we going to do about the black belt test?"

"I don't know. Sensei Teresa knows what the surprise is, but she wouldn't tell me. She says it's important."

"Riza's not going to change her mind," Denny said mournfully. "But I don't care! I'm not gong to Miami. I'm going to Key West and that's my final word."

Steven turned out the light. "Shut up and go to sleep. If you throw up, you're cleaning it up yourself."

Denny curled up around his cell phone, waiting in the darkness for a return message from Brian. Ocean waves broke quietly against the bow and out in the galley Steven started to snore, but the phone remained silent.

CHAPTER SIXTEEN

Brian was pretty sure he'd messed things up. No, he was dead certain he'd ruined them. He hadn't meant to be such a jerk to Denny, certainly hadn't intended to break up with him, but he'd opened his mouth and all those words had come out and it was just like red-hot lava spewing out of a volcano. Which was strange, because Brian didn't usually think of himself as a volcano kind of guy. He prided himself on being calm and steady, a rock.

Volcanoes were made of rock, though, he reminded himself.

And there was only so much heat a rock could take before it melted into bright boiling sludge.

"What did you say?" his mother asked, her gaze focused on the TV.

They were watching movies again, for the sixth night in a row. And they'd had room service for dinner again, for the sixth night in a row. She was sitting in her bathrobe steadily drinking wine, and he was sitting in an armchair slowly going insane.

Or maybe not slowly after all.

"I didn't say anything," Brian told his mother.

"Okay."

"I'll be back in a few minutes," he said.

He didn't even think she noticed when he left.

In his room, he flopped belly-down on his bed and glumly

considered his phone. Denny had sent him a message a few hours ago: *call me i'm sorry*. Except that Denny didn't really have anything to apologize for, right? He'd never wavered in his goal to go away into the military, and being homosexual was still against regulations even if the president was thinking of doing away with it.

Before he could stop himself, Brian hit the speed-dial for his old boyfriend, Christopher, up in Boston. On any normal summer night Christopher would be out with friends, either shopping or partying. Having his broken leg in a long, uncomfortable cast had put a damper on that.

"How's life in sun-drenched Florida?" Christopher asked when he answered.

"It's dark out," Brian replied. Despite the air-conditioning he'd opened the sliding glass door of the balcony. The warm breeze smelled not just of the ocean and seaweed but also of that thick topical earthiness that you couldn't get away from in Florida. "How's life in equally dark Massachusetts?"

"I'm sitting in my room when I should be out wasting my youth."

Brian rolled over on his back and stared at the ceiling. "How's your leg?"

"Hurts a lot, thanks. I'm going to probably have a limp for the rest of my life. Crippled Chris, they'll call me. I'll have to have a special shoe because one leg is so much shorter than the other."

Brian let the complaints wash over him like waves coming ashore. "Is that all you've got?"

"I'll never be able to bend it backward over a guy during sex again," Christopher added. "Happy?"

"No. I can't go to MIT in September."

Christopher screeched, "What?"

Brian moved the phone away from his ear to save his hearing. He pressed the speakerphone button. "The finances are all messed up because of my stepdad. I might have to take a year off and let things settle down. They do it in Europe all the time. Gap year."

"They do it so they can ride around on trains and sleep in rat-infested hostels and get drugs in Amsterdam," Christopher replied. "Notice I'm not opposed to the last part, but I don't see a Eurail pass in your future."

Brian felt wounded. "I could ride around Europe on a train!"

"You won't even ride the subway in Boston."

Which was true, sometimes, but only because he didn't like holding onto poles and touching handles that other people had left their germs all over. Not that he was a germophobe. Not much. Wintertime wasn't too bad. Even though someone was usually sniffling or sneezing, most everyone wore gloves. But in summer, people left their sweat and viruses and who-knew-what-else everywhere, a big sticky invisible film of disease.

Christopher said, "Is your mom telling you that you can't go to school?"

Brian watched the dark blades of the ceiling fan swirl around over his head. "She's not using those words."

"Which words is she using?"

"I'm trying not to listen."

"You can't take a year off," Christopher insisted. "You'll be bored and unhappy."

Which was possible, indeed probable, but it wasn't as if he had much of a choice—if the money wasn't there, the money wasn't there. It didn't grow on palm trees and it didn't wash ashore at high tide. MIT wasn't about to hand him a free ride just because his family's finances had all dried up.

"They must have students who have financial aid problems right before the term starts," Christopher insisted.

"This isn't a problem, it's a disaster," Brian replied.

Christopher was silent for a moment. Brian stayed quiet, too. He wanted to ask Christopher for advice about Denny, but that was an area he didn't dare go near.

Finally Christopher said, "If you can't go to school you should come up to Boston anyway, crash with us. Get a job and get out of Nowheresville."

"Sleep on your sofa and work in a coffee shop?" Brian asked. "Watch you go to BU all day while I make Frappucinos?"

"Yes!"

"I hate Frappucinos," Brian said. "And I can't leave my mom."

"She can't take care of things herself?"

"She shouldn't have to."

"You need to get out and get laid," Christopher said. "How's your ridiculously repressed hero boy?"

"I don't want to talk about him."

Christopher sounded gleeful. "Oh! Still crushing hopelessly, huh? He's never going to risk his macho military career for you."

"Still not talking."

"How about that other guy? What's his name? Works in the bookstore."

Brian didn't remember Christopher going anywhere near the Bookmine when he'd been visiting. Christopher and books did not mix. "You mean Sean?"

"Sean, yeah, whatever. Do him."

That wasn't going to happen. Sean was cute in his own way, and kind of smart-alecky, but Christopher didn't feel any kind of spark when he thought about him. Still, after he hung up with Christopher he texted Sean a message.

Need your advice, he sent.

No response came back. Brian wished he wasn't so alone in his life, or so alone in this room. Thinking about Denny—handsome, strong, ridiculously athletic, tanned—made him feel even more sorry for himself. He went out to the suite's living room but his mother had turned off the TV and gone to her own room. The light was still on behind the closed door.

He knocked. "Mom? You okay?"

"Come on in," she said.

Brian entered carefully. She was sitting on the edge of her bed, holding a framed picture taken when they'd first moved to Fisher Key over the winter. Mom and Henrik were smiling widely, and Brian was standing in the middle with a more somber look. He remembered that day. The real estate agent had tried to cajole him into smiling, but he'd resented moving down from Massachusetts.

"Everything was supposed to be wonderful for us down here," Mom said, her eyes bright but her voice steady. "You make plans, and you have hopes, and then everything goes wrong."

"Not everything," Brian said.

"Everything," she repeated. With a sigh, she put the picture aside and gave him a direct look. "But when we make a mess, we clean it up. I'm not your responsibility, Brian."

He hadn't moved from the doorway. "I know that."

"I don't think you do," she said sadly. "This is your time. You've worked hard in school, you've had your hopes set on MIT for years, and we're going to figure out this financial aid problem. But even if the worst happens and you have to defer one semester—semester, not year—you don't have to babysit me."

Brian's face felt warm. He knew he was blushing. "You heard what I said to Christopher."

Mom stood, crossed the room, and gave him a hug. She still smelled like wine, and he wasn't sure she was sober. But it felt nice to get a hug. It reminded him of the days before Henrik, when it had been just the two of them against the world.

"You're going to live your life and I'm going to live mine," she said. "We'll figure this out."

When he returned to his room, he turned off the lights and crawled into bed. The patio door was still open. He could hear the Gulf of Mexico washing up gently on the tiny beach below, and distant lights revealed boats on the water. Brian didn't check his phone again. Instead he curled around a pillow and wondered where Denny was and what he was thinking.

In the morning, when he checked his messages, he saw exactly what Denny had been thinking.

"Hey, Mom," he said, as she drank steadily from a tall glass of orange juice. "Do you care if I go to Key West for the weekend?"

CHAPTER SEVENTEEN

The second day of diving with Brad and Tristan started out better, at least as far as Steven was concerned. For starters, they showed up on time. Brad didn't seem to notice that Denny was quiet and hiding behind sunglasses. If Tristan noticed signs of a hangover, she didn't say anything.

Steven, on the other hand, was more than delighted to talk extra-loud around Denny, and to eat two greasy sausage-muffin combos in front of him, and generally irritate him any way possible.

"Get away from me before I toss you into the ocean," Denny growled when Steven followed him up to the wheelhouse.

"What? Am I bothering your delicate constitution?"

"I'll bother you with a punch in the face."

Steven decided to temporarily retreat, if only to plan more irritation for later on.

Tristan holed up down in the galley, reading her astronomy book again. Pouring coffee for himself, Steven asked, "Is that what you're going to study? Astronomy?"

"Astrophysics," she said.

"Same difference."

"Hardly."

"What, you sit in a lab staring at a computer all day instead of sitting in an observatory staring at the sky? How's that going to improve the world?"

Tristan flipped the page. "Is that what you think we should all do? Improve the world?"

"Sure. Why not?"

"Because it gets you blown up," she said. "Or shot, or killed, or paralyzed from the waist down."

Steven sipped the coffee. Hot and black, but not as bitter as she sounded. "Is that how your dad feels about it?"

"No, it's my own opinion."

"It's a pretty sucky one."

"Says you," Tristan replied. "Matthew and I feel differently."

"Who's Matthew? Your boyfriend?"

"Yes."

Steven asked, "What's the point of living your life if you're not going to make a difference?"

"I can make a difference by discovering the origin of the universe," she said. "What does the military do to better the world? By its very definition, war is all about death and destruction. You're not saving the village, you're burning it down."

"The military helps people get rid of dictators and torturers," Steven said. "What are you, a pacifist?"

"It's possible to change the world through non-violence. Look what Gandhi did. And Martin Luther King."

Steven made a gagging noise. "Sorry. I always get nauseated in the face of blind idealism. You know what happened to Gandhi and King? They got shot."

"Is your girlfriend as militant as you?" Tristan asked.

Steven had forgotten his little white lie. Had he told her he was dating Kelsey or Jen? He said, "Militant or not, when someone's got a gun pointed at someone I love, non-violence is the least likely option I'm going to go for."

"Which is why you and I are never going to be on the same page," she said.

And thank goodness for that, not if her page was full of abstract science and impractical views of the world. Steven had met too many criminals to believe in touchy-feely justice, and knew too many good soldiers and lawmakers to think their occupation was all about destruction.

He went back on deck to check over their gear, and was surprised when Brad asked, "Tristan getting your goat?"

"What? No."

"She does," Brad said, very casual about it. "She likes to rile people up. And I say that as someone who loves her."

Steven squinted against the sun. They had several more minutes before they reached Rum Reef, and he supposed making nice with Brad made good business sense. "She doesn't like the military."

"She holds a grudge," Brad admitted. "She gives my brother a hard time, too, saying the Coast Guard should stick to poachers."

"It doesn't sound like she knows much about what they do," Steven said, thinking about all the things that would be required of Denny at school: learning seamanship, law enforcement, and rules of international waters.

Brad turned over his camera and inspected the battery pack. "We all have our blind spots."

Steven didn't know if that was supposed to be an apology for the argument yesterday, but he was willing to take it as one. They sat in companionable silence, inspecting the regulators and hoses, while the *Idle* carried them farther from shore. A glint on the horizon proved to be the Coast Guard, accompanied by the *Othello I* and *Othello II*. Steven had noticed the *Othello II* leaving port early that morning.

"I guess they still haven't found their satellite," he said.

Brad asked, "Who?"

"A contractor named Othello Industries," Steven said. "Ever hear of them?"

The older man looked thoughtful for a moment. "Maybe, once or twice. Nothing that stands out very much. Like a lot of defense companies, they were hurt by the dismantling of the space shuttle program. What kind of satellite?"

"They say it was a weather gauge."

Brad shook his head. "Weather satellites aren't designed to survive reentry through the atmosphere. If they're looking for something sturdy enough for that, it's not going to be carrying weather information."

"I knew it!" Steven said. "What could it be?"

"Military intelligence, probably. Nothing for kids to worry about."

Steven scowled at him, but Brad only smirked and went back to checking his equipment.

By nine thirty they were moored near Rum Reef and the remains of a Civil War wreck. They had the whole site to themselves. Denny didn't volunteer to go into the water and Steven wasn't heartless enough to make him, so he went under with Tristan and Brad. Visibility was even better today than yesterday. Steven wished he'd brought his own camera along. He liked the way the light rippled around them, and the big white and pink sea fans, and the plants that rippled in the current.

Tristan was wearing a yellow bikini today under her BC. She was all curves and smooth skin. Steven kept himself from looking at her. The nice thing about Jen was she had no opinions about the military, and the nice thing about Kelsey was she was a pragmatist. Tristan seemed like one of those uppity intellectuals who were happy to criticize the military until they themselves were in jeopardy. He hated people like that.

A sleek young dolphin darted by them, followed by a larger one. A mom and her kid playing around. Steven didn't see the rest of the pod, but they were somewhere nearby. Tristan grinned behind her mask as the dolphins made another sweep. Steven smiled back, entirely by reflex, before he caught himself and stopped.

He didn't like her, and he wasn't about to start liking her. In three days she'd be out of his life and on her snooty way to college, which was absolutely fine with him.

❖

Denny's new phone didn't get reception this far from land, but that didn't stop him from checking it out of habit. He was trying to forget his headache and the slow roll his stomach did every now and then. Coffee helped, and more aspirin, and boy, he was never again drinking three beers (or maybe it had been four, he wasn't quite sure) on a mostly empty stomach after a day of scuba diving and a night of having the roof fall in.

He'd been alone for about twenty minutes on the *Idle* when his stomach lurched again. But this wasn't the hangover speaking. The wind had kicked up, bringing choppy waves. He scanned the horizon, noting an increase in clouds, and checked the weather radio. The forecast for a mostly sunny day had changed for the worse.

Steven, Tristan, and Brad returned on schedule. Tristan talked excited about dolphins but Steven's gaze had already gone to the darkening sky.

"Weather's turning bad," Denny said. "We're going to have to turn back."

Brad asked, "What? For a little rain?"

"A lot of rain, according to the marine forecast," Denny said. "Sorry."

Brad grumbled and Tristan looked disappointed, but soon the clouds were directly overhead and the first raindrops had started to patter down. Steven suggested they carry Brad below but he insisted a little water wasn't going to hurt him. Tristan stayed with him on the bench, both of them huddled under a tarp and outfitted with life preservers, as Steven kept watch and Denny brought the *Idle* back to Fisher Key.

"What are we supposed to do for the rest of the day?" Brad complained as they hauled his camera and gear back to his van.

"You could head down to Key West," Steven suggested. "The Fisher Museum's kind of interesting."

The words *Key West* triggered a vague memory for Denny. Something about a hotel? He had left his phone back up in the wheelhouse. When he checked it, he found a voice mail had come in while they'd been out at sea.

"Okay," Brian said in the message. "I'd love to. Mom'll be okay if I'm gone for a night or two."

Denny had no idea what he was talking about. Love to what? Gone where? Uneasy, he checked his phone log. He'd sent Brian a message that he didn't even remember:

come to key west weekend
for my test please make it special
stay sat night nice hotel
miss you please come.

He groaned and thumped his head against the nearest bulkhead.

What was he going to tell his parents and Aunt Riza now?

CHAPTER EIGHTEEN

The rain cleared out, but strong winds and a cloudy forecast ruled out a trip back to sea. Denny and Steven swung by the house to see if there was anything they could do to help. Dad was there, eating lunch while leaning against the hood of his police cruiser. Roofers were up on top of the house and a portable storage pod had been put on the lawn for the furniture the workers were carrying out.

"If I'd known you were coming I would have brought extra sandwiches," Dad said.

Denny's stomach grumbled at the smell of tuna fish. "Weather forced us back. I'll give you a silver dollar for half of your sandwich."

Dad jerked his thumb toward the front seat. "How about some potato chips for free?"

Denny grabbed the large bag of chips. Dad wasn't acting mad or weird about dinner last night, which was good. But he didn't yet know about the monumental mistake Denny had made with his phone.

"Any mail come in?" Steven asked, and Denny knew exactly what he was looking for: that waiver for BUD/S.

"Nothing," Dad said. "Sorry."

Denny offered him a consolation potato chip.

Steven took it and then squinted at the workers and asked, "Is that my dresser?"

"They're clearing out your whole room," Dad said. "The carpet's coming out, too. Your room and mine."

Denny said, "What about all our stuff?"

"I pulled out what I could," Dad said. "Water damaged a lot, and there's mold, too. Guess there's been a slow leak for a while now. You'll both need new mattresses and box springs."

"Do we really?" Steven asked.

Dad asked, confused, "You want to sleep on the floor?"

"No, I mean he's going away and I'm going away eventually." Steven grabbed the bag of chips and ate a large one. "You could turn our room into, I don't know. A sewing room?"

"Who in this family sews?" Denny asked, frowning.

"Or a guest room," Steven proposed.

Denny took the chips back. "I want my room back."

"Don't be a baby," Steven said. "You're going to spend most of the next four years away, and you'll be back only on vacations."

Dad finished his sandwich. "And you?"

Steven shrugged. "If I don't get my waiver, I could move out and get an apartment somewhere."

Sometimes Denny just didn't understand what was going on in his brother's head. "An apartment. With who? Eddie?"

"You don't have to sound like it's the stupidest idea in the world," Steven said, his gaze narrowing.

"But it is," Denny said. "Unless you're going to pay his rent for him. Besides, your waiver's going to come through."

Steven grunted but didn't say anything. Dad sipped from a can of soda and watched the workers. Gulls fought over something on the shore of the lagoon, their wings flapping angrily.

"How's Mom today?" Denny asked.

"Happily going through carpet samples," Dad said. "You'd think this tree falling in was the best thing that ever happened."

Steven said, "And Aunt Riza?"

"Is still herself," Dad said succinctly.

Denny said, "Steven, why don't you go see if there's anything left in our room we should have?"

Steven ate the last potato chip and crumpled up the bag. "Like what?"

Denny replied, clearly and slowly, "I don't know. That's why you should go check."

"Oh," Steven said, switching his gaze from Denny to Dad and back again. "Whatever."

Steven ambled off toward the house. Denny waited until he was out of earshot before saying, "I kind of made a mistake last night."

Dad's eyebrows arched. "Is this a I-have-to-arrest-you kind of mistake?"

"No! I sorta maybe invited Brian to come down with me to Key West for the black belt test. And to spend the weekend." Denny didn't dare look at his father. "And I know, this whole thing with Aunt Riza's not settled, but I was kind of not thinking, and it sort of…just came out. And he wants to go, and you know what? I only have twenty days left before I go away, and I want to do this."

"Huh," Dad said.

The wind picked up, tugging at the roof tarp. One of the roofers nailed down a loose corner. Denny waited for Dad to say more but nothing came.

Denny asked, "Is that it?"

"I guess," Dad said.

Denny squinted at him. Dad had that inscrutable expression on his face, the one he used most often with criminal suspects and people undergoing police interrogation.

"You're thinking that I got myself into this mess so I need to get myself out of it," Denny said.

"More or less."

"But I really want to take this test," Denny insisted. "And we had it scheduled first. It's totally unfair for Aunt Riza to have a party the same day."

Dad said, "A party for *you*, kiddo."

"I didn't ask for one."

"Sometimes family does stuff for us without even asking," Dad said, just as his radio came to life in the cruiser. "Because they love us."

That was a crummy thing to say, because it was true. And Denny knew what he had to do, even if it wasn't what he wanted to do. He listened to the dispatcher tell Dad about a car accident up on the Overseas Highway and moved away from the cruiser.

"On my way," Dad said to the dispatcher. Then, to Denny, "I'll see you both later, okay?"

"Okay," Denny said.

Steven returned a few minutes later, clutching some soggy paperbacks and his favorite running shirt. "This is all I could find. Did you tell Dad whatever's bothering you that you couldn't tell me?"

"It's nothing," Denny sighed, but shared the story of the drunken text message.

"Ha." Steven got into his truck and turned the ignition. "I knew I should have taken your phone away from you. What are we going to do about the test?"

Denny climbed into the passenger side. "You're going to go to Key West and I'm going to go to Miami."

"That's what Dad said?"

"No. That's what I'm going to tell Mom. A compromise."

"And Brian?"

"Will maybe forgive me." At least, Denny hoped that he would.

Steven turned onto the road. He was quiet for a half mile, his hands tight on the wheel. Then he said, "I'm not taking it without you. Sensei Mike will postpone it if we ask."

"Who knows when we'll both be back at the same time," Denny replied.

Steven's grip tightened. "You say that like I have someplace to go."

"The waiver—"

"Isn't here, and maybe isn't coming," Steven said tightly.

"There's other things you could do in the military besides be a SEAL."

"Not for me," Steven said.

"Because you're an idiot," Denny said. "You could be a Coast Guard rescue swimmer. Is that so terrible, pulling drowning people out of the water? I know there's usually no explosions or bombs, but maybe you could overlook that in favor of, I don't know, *saving lives*."

"Shut up."

"And there's no guns for you to shoot, but oh, yeah, *saving lives*—"

Steven reached over and punched his arm. "What if I had to work for someone like you? I'd throw myself into the Arctic Ocean."

"And then maybe you could rescue yourself, *saving a life*—"

Denny's campaign ended ten seconds later when Steven pulled into the parking lot of the Bookmine. They looked through the front windows to where Aunt Riza was working the counter, no doubt haranguing customers into spending more than they'd intended.

"You need backup?" Steven asked.

"No," Denny said. "I need a hamburger with extra-large fries. And onion rings, too."

"I'll be back in fifteen."

Once Denny was inside, he went directly to Mom's office. She was bent over the computer keyboard, laboriously clicking on the yellowed keys.

"You should follow my advice and get a new computer," Denny said.

"All computers hate me." Mom's glare at the screen softened when she glanced up. "Why aren't you out at sea?"

"Rain." Denny closed the door behind him and sat in a chair already crowded with piles of books. "I have to talk to you about this party."

Mom wheeled her chair back from the cramped computer desk. Her dress today was full of orange and yellow flowers. "I don't think I'm the one you have to talk to."

"I'll go," he said. "If Steven can go take the test. That's fair, isn't it?"

Mom gazed at him for a long moment. "Is that what you want?"

"Yes," he said. "That's exactly what I want."

She stood up, knocked on the glass window separating her office from the front counter, and motioned for Aunt Riza to join them.

CHAPTER NINETEEN

The Li'l Conch Café was jammed full of customers. Steven grabbed a stool at the end of the counter, put in his order to go, and checked his phone. Jen and Kelsey had both left messages. He didn't listen to them. A familiar laugh made him turn sideways. Sean Garrity and Brian Vandermark were sitting in a corner booth, with Sean laughing and Brian ducking his head shyly.

Oh. So not good.

Steven turned back before either of them could see him. He hadn't known they were friends. Hadn't realized they were the kind of friends to go to lunch together and tell jokes and smile shyly. He wondered if Denny knew about it. He didn't want to be the one to tell him.

An elderly man and woman wearing NASA ball caps took the stools beside Steven.

"I hear this is the best food on the island," the man said. "That true?"

"Completely true," Steven said. "You like NASA?"

"We're retired from it," said the woman. She was silver-haired and trim, her cheeks bright from the sun.

"Got our gold watches," said the man.

The woman added, "And two pensions."

Her name was Irma and his name was Ed. They'd started

work way back when the place was called Cape Canaveral, which had changed to Cape Kennedy, and then eventually changed back again, except for the parts that were still the Kennedy Space Center. Neither of their jobs had been very glamorous. Supply, requisitions, and procurement, they said. They were very proud of all those astronauts and the thousands of people that had made each mission possible.

Ed said, "We've seen every single space shuttle launch."

"All we have to do is set up folding chairs in our driveway," Irma said.

Louanne Garrity came over to take their order. Ed wanted a chili dog and Irma asked for a grilled cheese sandwich with tomatoes.

"I hear NASA just lost a satellite in the ocean," Steven said, when Louanne was gone.

Ed shook his head glumly. "Countries are always losing stuff. Russia, India, China—all of them. You never know what's going to come falling down next."

Sean Garrity laughed loudly again. Steven risked a glance. Sean and Brian were sliding out of their booth.

"They say it was a weather satellite, but a friend of mine says those wouldn't survive reentry," Steven said.

Irma looked thoughtful. "Depends on how big it was. If it's the size of a bus it might."

Ed said, "Or maybe even a minivan."

Steven leaned forward, both elbows on the counter. "I met some people who are looking for this one. They work for some company called Othello."

"Ha!" Ed said. "Dirty top to bottom."

Irma pinched the back of his wrinkled hand. "You can't say that."

"Dealt with them all the time," Ed said.

"One year," Irma corrected. "Our last year."

Steven said, "Not a good experience, huh?"

"They were always within the letter of the law," Irma said, "if not the exact spirit of it. What makes a young man like you so interested?"

Steven shrugged. "I think it's kind of cool, some satellite lying in the ocean out there."

Irma said. "Good luck to you if you go looking for it. Like a needle in a haystack. An ocean haystack."

Sean and Brian reached the cash register. Steven tried to slouch and remain inconspicuous, but Brian saw him and did a double take. For a moment, he maybe thought Steven was Denny.

Would serve you right to get caught, Steven thought.

Louanne Garrity brought over Steven's lunch order and put the paper bag down in front of him with perhaps more force than was strictly necessary. "I hear you've been ducking Melissa Hardy."

"What?" Steven asked. "Says who?"

Louanne took his money. "Says Melissa. You said Saturday night that you were going to call her."

"A tree fell on my house!" Steven argued. "I've been kind of busy ever since."

"It's already Tuesday," Louanne said. "That's like ten years in Fisher Key time. So call her. She's really nice and you've had a crush on her ever since we were two grades ahead of you in school, right?"

"Right," Steven said, and fled with the lunch bag.

He ate most of his fries on the short drive back to the Bookmine. From the vantage point of the parking lot he could see Robin at the counter, but no sign of Denny, their mom, or Aunt Riza. He figured the decent thing to do would be wade in there and support his twin. The hamburgers smelled delicious, though, and he was absolutely starving.

Denny was a big boy. He could take care of himself against two short Cuban women, blood relatives or not.

❖

"Absolutely not," Aunt Riza said. "Your brother must attend the party as well! It would be disrespectful not to."

Denny stared at her. "Disrespectful to who?"

She waved her hand. "To you!"

Mom squeezed the bridge of her nose and made a suffering sound.

Denny had tried patiently explaining why it would be an insult to Sensei Mike for both of them to cancel. He'd hoped she would understand how important the black belt test was to them. True to his expectations, though, she brushed off his concerns. Which left the compromise, which she was also rejecting.

"I won't be insulted." Denny's voice rose with agitation. He fought to bring it down. "I promise."

"It's not acceptable," Aunt Riza said.

"Ree," Mom said, "we've talked about this. You could move it to Sunday and no one would object."

"You could?" Denny asked.

Aunt Riza blinked owlishly at them both. "Saturday is a much better day, astrologically speaking."

"Astrology is just superstition," Denny said.

Mom gave him a look that clearly said he wasn't helping himself.

Denny turned back to his aunt. "If you can move it to Sunday, then Steven and I can take our black belt test, and you'll make us doubly happy. We can come up to Miami knowing we achieved one of our biggest goals in life, just like you've also worked to achieve your own goals."

"I've worked very hard," Aunt Riza acknowledged. She folded her hands in her lap. "People don't realize."

Denny sensed he was on the track to victory. "It means everything to us that you want to have a party. This one little thing, moving it to Sunday, would make us grateful forever."

Aunt Riza sighed. "I think you're too persuasive."

Denny said, "Is that a good thing?"

"If I move it to Sunday," she said. "And you and your brother will be happy, and you'll dress nicely, and you won't bring your friend."

Denny's mouth opened and slammed shut again. He hadn't even thought about bringing Brian. Now that she mentioned it, though, how was he going to explain to Brian that he'd promised a romantic weekend but was now ditching him?

A headache began to blossom behind his eyes.

"What do you think, Denny?" His mother asked. Both women were gazing at him expectantly.

"I won't bring anyone," Denny murmured.

The thrill of victory was immediately replaced by the ashen taste of failure. He couldn't believe he'd just agreed to that. He trudged out of the store and into the parking lot, wondering if he should just throw himself in front of traffic. Steven's truck was out there, though, and the jerk was eating lunch without him.

"Brian will understand," Steven said when Denny told him the deal.

Denny slowly banged his head against the dashboard. "No, he won't. I'm such a jerk."

Steven offered the lunch. "Here. Have some of your fries. Ask me what I learned about the missing satellite."

Denny groaned. "I don't care about the missing satellite."

"Don't you have any curiosity at all?"

"No."

"It's really small."

Denny ate some fries. "So's your brain."

"Hey, I'm not the one who just made a bad deal."

"Is it really bad?" Denny asked plaintively. "Did I just make a huge mistake?"

"I don't know," Steven said. "You'll know when you tell Brian."

CHAPTER TWENTY

I am so sick of room service," Brian said over the phone. "Can we go out to dinner somewhere? I don't care where."

It wasn't the romantic dinner that Denny had planned back on Saturday night, but he borrowed his dad's car again, put on the only decent shorts and shirt he had, and drove Brian down to a Marathon seafood restaurant named Leia's. The place was crammed full of mermaid statues, fishing nets, and old photos of the bomber training strip that was now the airport. The patio overlooked the Atlantic. The breeze was still strong enough to flap the colorful pirate flags hanging from the poles.

"I like this place," Brian said. "It's got character."

Denny squeezed lemon into his iced tea. "Lots."

"You okay? You've been quiet since you picked me up."

"Yes. Fine."

Brian simply gazed at him.

Denny shifted on his seat. "You have to promise not to get mad at me."

"I can't promise that," Brian said slowly. "What is it?"

Denny reached for sugar next. Deliberately he tore open a packet, poured the contents into his tea, and stirred it slowly. "I have to reschedule this weekend to next weekend."

"Oh," Brian replied. "Why?"

The waitress walked by with a large party of tourists and sat them in a corner of the patio. Brian was momentarily distracted. Denny took the opportunity to check out the expression on his face. Not mad. Not mad *yet*.

"My aunt is throwing some family party up in Miami, and Mom says we have to go," Denny said.

Brian tilted his head. "So why would I get upset?"

"Because this is our chance to get away," Denny said, feeling miserable. "And I'd rather spend time with you than seeing a bunch of stuffy old relatives."

"But we can go the weekend after," Brian said, still not upset. "It's not a big deal. Can I still watch you take your black belt test on Saturday?"

"It's going to be all day long, and really boring."

"I won't be bored." Brian reached over the table, patted Denny's arm, and quickly withdrew his hand. "Promise."

Denny barely had a moment to enjoy that brief contact, skin on skin. Not that he was obsessing, but the countdown in his head was flashing big red numbers at him. Twenty days until he went away. Twenty days and all he and Brian had done was kiss a few times, plus some groping on the lumpy sofa in the apartment.

"If you put any more sugar in that tea you're going to turn diabetic," Brian said.

Denny glanced in surprise at the torn sugar packets on the table. He only remembered opening one. "Maybe I better order something else to drink," he said sheepishly.

For dinner, Brian had the Cuban Mix sandwich and Denny ordered a steak. He didn't think he'd get much steak at the academy. He didn't imagine he'd be sitting on a patio overlooking the ocean anytime soon after Reporting In Day, either. When he tried to picture his life twenty days into the future, it was a big blank ocean of the unknown—exciting and terrifying at the same time.

But Brian's future was that same confusing mix, Denny

reminded himself. Worse, because of the uncertainty of coming up with the tuition money, and getting to MIT.

"How's the financial aid thing going?" Denny asked. "Any news?"

Brian's gaze was out on the ocean, where some tourists were Jet-Skiing in the final hour before sunset. "No news from the school. Mom says that at worst, I'll miss one term while we get it straightened out and I could start in January."

"Would you stay down here until then?" Denny asked.

The Jet-Skiers zoomed around each other—two guys and a younger woman, all of them laughing and shouting encouragement to each other. Brian said, "I don't know. Christopher says I could stay up there in Boston, sleep on his couch."

Denny didn't like Christopher, even though he'd only known him for a few days. And he didn't like Brian talking to him, even though that was a jealous and totally irrational response.

"Do you want to sleep on his couch?" Denny asked carefully.

"Absolutely not," Brian said vehemently.

Denny smiled. "Good. You deserve at least a futon."

After dinner they sat in Dad's car at the end of Leia's parking lot and kissed some more. And this was the absolute highlight of Denny's day, because Brian smelled great and his mouth was warm and firm, and he kissed Denny like he was special. Wherever his hands went, Denny's skin warmed and wanted more.

Brian's hands went to his shoulders, his back, and then lower—

"Help!" a woman yelled out, a distant cry on the water.

Denny jerked back from Brian's arms. He saw people running to the water's edge, which was lined with moss-covered rocks. The bystanders pointed out into the water but no one made a move to get into the ocean.

"What is it?" Brian asked.

They got out of the car to see what was going on. One of the

Jet Skis had capsized several dozen yards offshore. Its operator was floating in the water. One of the man's friends had slowed down to help and was in danger of capsizing his own machine. The third rider, the woman, was making circles and yelling for assistance.

"What are you—you can't go in there," Brian said as Denny pulled off his shirt.

"Sure I can." Denny toed off his sandals, too, and pressed his cell phone into Brian's hand. "Call nine-one-one!"

It wasn't a far swim, not compared to what he normally did, but the choppy waves and diminishing light slowed him. The stricken man was fifty or so years old, heavyset, his eyes closed and his lips blue. His friend had abandoned his own Jet Ski and was trying to pound his back, but life vests hindered them both.

"Come on, Fred! Breathe!" the friend yelled.

Fred showed no signs of life. Denny knew they didn't have time to wait for more help.

"Hold on to your machine," Denny told him. "I'll get him to shore."

He started rescue breathing. He didn't have a portable mask with him, not even a disposable plastic shield, so he had to put his mouth over Fred's cold lips and force air into him. The man's mouth reeked of alcohol.

"Oh, that's nasty," Denny said.

He couldn't do compressions, not with the vest in place, so he alternated breathing and towing Fred toward shore. Breathe, tow, breathe, tow.

After four rounds of that, Fred started to cough and choke and flail.

"Easy, don't fight!" Denny told him. Panicking victims could drag a rescuer down. "I've got you. Just breathe."

"What's what?" Fred asked. "Huh?"

"Let me do the work," Denny said.

Fred stopped jerking his arms, but he continued to cough and sputter. Everything had gone dark now except for the yellow and white lanterns on the restaurant patio. Denny was maybe thirty feet from shore when a fire truck arrived with spinning red lights. Two firefighters waded into the waves while others held up flashlights.

"Good job, Anderson," said one of the firefighters as they took Fred from him. "Nice to see you again without a tree on your head."

The firefighters helped Denny ashore. He wasn't tired, much, but the currents had been stronger than he expected, and he was shivering. Someone got a blanket around his shoulders and then Brian was there, holding the edges for him. Brian also had Denny's shirt and sandals.

"Are you okay?" Brian demanded.

"Yeah." Denny spat out some seawater and took his shirt from Brian's hands. "Just wet."

"You can't stop being a hero," Brian said, with both fondness and exasperation.

Denny hoped that meant some more kissing in the car tonight. "I guess not."

The ambulance crew got Fred onto a gurney. The firefighters helped Fred's friend out of the water. The friend said, "Just like that! He keeled over, no reason," and Denny smelled the booze on his breath, too.

"No reason at all, huh?" asked Sgt. Bonnie Powell, who'd responded to the call. Denny had known her for years. He was happy that his father hadn't shown up on the call. Dad deserved a night off. Powell asked, "How much have you had to drink tonight, sir?"

"Nothing! I swear!" Fred's friend seized Denny's hand in an anxious grip. "You're a lifesaver, kid. He'd be dead and I'd be explaining to his wife—"

The rest of the sentence was cut off by the man leaning forward and choking. No, not choking. Vomiting. Denny was just one second too late in moving out of the way, and he paid for his slow reaction.

"Oh, gross," Brian said, from safely out of range.

"I think I drank too much," Fred's friend said.

Denny stared down at the ruined towel. And his balled-up shirt. And his shorts. Even his feet were covered with vomit. He didn't think there'd be any more kissing until he got a hot shower. And maybe a bath in disinfectant.

Sgt. Powell looked around. "Someone get a bucket of water!"

"Tell your friend he's welcome," Denny said.

CHAPTER TWENTY-ONE

Steven heard footsteps on the deck above him. Denny appeared on the steps, wearing a Fisher Key police T-shirt and carrying his sandals.

"How was your date?" Steven asked. "And why do you smell so bad?"

"Because I'm a stupid Good Samaritan." Denny surveyed the trash bags surrounding Steven, all of them stuffed with damp or ruined clothes from the house. "What are you doing?"

"Black belt test on Saturday, right?"

"Right."

"And what are we going to wear during the black belt test?"

"We're going to wear our..." Denny sat down on the galley bench. "Uniforms?"

"Start digging," Steven said.

They found their white karate uniforms, or gis, in the bottom of one bag lumped with some muddy towels and ripped blue jeans. The mud had soaked into the white fabric and the result wasn't pretty.

"I'm thinking a bottle or two of bleach," Steven said.

Denny squinted skeptically. "Optimist."

"Got any quarters?"

The marina had a small Laundromat, but the convenience store was closed. Steven resigned himself to driving into town. Then he saw that the *Othello II* was back in port. It must have come in while he was busy sorting through ruined clothes. Bud, the guy with the Red Sox hat, was hosing off the top deck. Steven asked if he could borrow any bleach.

"Yeah, I think we've got some," Bud said, and went below.

He was gone for several minutes. Steven was about to give up when Claire emerged on deck. She was dressed up in a skirt and pretty green blouse, and had an industrial-sized plastic bottle in her hands.

"Laundry at this time of night?" she asked.

"Can't wait another day," Steven said. "Going out?"

"Hoping to," Claire said. "The engine's busted again. I won that bet, so Bud owes me a cheeseburger."

"Bud?" Steven asked. "Not Harrison?"

She gave him a sunny smile. "Jamie's got his own plans. Don't be jealous. I'm too old to be your type."

"You're not old," Steven protested, a flush blossoming on his face. If she let him take off her blouse he'd show her that he wasn't some naïve kid. If she let him take off more, he'd happily forget all his plans of staying away from women all summer.

"You're cute," Claire said, and that was like a knife to the heart. Puppies were cute. Kittens were cute. Steven was not a puppy or kitten. Claire continued, "Any recommendation for burgers?"

He ducked his gaze. "The Li'l Conch Café. Can't beat it."

"Excellent," she said. "Here's the bleach. Have fun."

Sitting in the Laundromat, watching the laundry machine spin and slosh water, he wondered how Tristan and her father had enjoyed their afternoon in Key West. Not that he cared what she was doing right now. He wasn't even thinking about her. He pulled out his phone and debated calling Melissa Hardy, like he'd promised. Or Jen or Kelsey, who'd both sent new text messages. Or the recruiter in Miami, Master Chief King, who certainly wouldn't be in the office right now, but how about that waiver, huh?

You're cute, Claire had said.

Two thorough washings over the next hour didn't get the stains out. Steven tried to figure out where they would get new uniforms in the next three days, considering the nearest martial arts store was up in Homestead. He put the ruined ones in the dryer anyway and went back down to the *Idle*. Denny had showered and was on the phone with Dad.

"He was only maybe fifty feet out," Denny was saying. "Not any trouble at all."

Dad said something Steven couldn't hear.

Denny replied, "Okay. I will."

Steven snagged an apple from the refrigerator. When Denny hung up, he asked, "Who was only fifty feet out?"

"Some drunk guy who dumped his Jet Ski," Denny replied.

"You help him?"

"No, I let him drown. Where are the uniforms?"

"Bad news. One of us is going to have to drive up to Homestead and get new ones."

Denny scowled. "Brad hired us until Friday afternoon. They'll be closed on a Friday night."

"Maybe Eddie could go up for us."

"He'd screw it up."

"You don't have to be so negative."

"I'm not negative." Denny grabbed some of the garbage bags. "But he'd mess it up somehow."

"When you come up with a better plan, let me know," Steven said.

It was Denny's turn to sleep in the galley bed. After stowing away the bags of clothes, he converted the table and benches and then flopped down on his pillow. He mumbled something about just one night's good rest. Steven waited another half hour before he went to retrieve the uniforms out of the dryer. He liked the marina at night—the softly lapping waves, all the boaters tucked in their beds, even the seagulls quiet. Fisher Key itself was a flat low profile under the stars, and he imagined how quiet it must have been a hundred years ago, or maybe two hundred years ago, when the only occupants had been some Spanish fishermen, escaped slaves, and Native Americans.

The laundry room was empty except for some flies buzzing around the fluorescent lights. As he folded the uniforms he watched through the window as a dark van pulled into the parking lot. Because of the angle, Steven couldn't see the plates or the driver. It sat there, idling, muffled music playing inside. Hard rock, maybe, not something he liked. After a moment or two, the van started rolling forward. The side door slid open, and a man fell out—no, not fell, was pushed, was pushed *hard*, and he tumbled down to the asphalt and didn't move.

The van peeled off. Steven sprinted across the lot and dropped down to a crouch.

"Hey, are you all right?"

A muffled curse, and the man sat up on his own—carefully, holding his right elbow. Steven recognized him in the dim parking lot lighting.

Jamie Harrison.

With a bloodied lip, too, and his clothes were rumpled, his face foul. He smelled like beer but didn't seem drunk.

"What are you doing out here?" Harrison asked.

"Neighborhood watch. Why are guys pushing you out of a van?"

Harrison spat blood on the ground. "I wasn't pushed. I fell out."

Steven stood skeptically. "Gravity is a killer, huh?"

Harrison hauled himself upright. He didn't sway, exactly, but it was clear that more than just his arm was hurting him. "Leave it alone, kid. None of your business."

Which was true in all sorts of ways, surely, but Steven had never been good at quelling his curiosity. Especially when people called him "kid."

"You owe them money?" he asked.

"No, I don't owe anyone money," Harrison retorted.

He was a jerk, and he probably deserved whatever had happened to him in the van, but Steven's father had always said the law was for everyone, not just the people you liked.

"My dad can help," Steven said. "He's a cop."

"Oh, yes, because that's exactly what I need," Harrison bit out, swinging around. "Isn't that perfect? Here you are, playing junior detective, playing around on your little boat, the whole world waiting for you. You've got it made, don't you?"

Steven blinked. "That's what you think?"

Harrison took three steps forward with a knowing smirk. "Oh, I know it. You think you've got the whole thing worked out, right? Never left home and never been on your own, but you've figured out all the secrets of life."

Steven forced his hands to stay flat against his legs and his voice to stay steady. "The secret is not to get pushed out of a van."

Harrison laughed. Not a nice sound. "Yeah. That's it."

He turned and walked off. Steven debated following him. It figured that something was shady about the guy. He'd sensed it from the beginning. But that didn't mean he should get involved. Better just to make sure that none of it spilled over in the marina or on people that he liked.

Steven retrieved the uniforms and watched Harrison go down and board his ship.

"I'm watching you," Steven murmured.

Of course Harrison couldn't hear him. But he turned back anyway, maybe sensing Steven's eyes on him, and for a long moment didn't move.

They might have stayed that way for hours, locked and staring, but finally Harrison went aboard his boat and took his secrets with him.

CHAPTER TWENTY-TWO

A ringing phone dragged Denny out of sleep the next morning. The ringtone was a Toby Keith song. Denny hated Toby Keith.

"Steven, answer that," he groaned.

No answer. More ringing. Stupid phone. Denny stumbled out of bed and groped around on the galley counter, where Steven had left his phone plugged in for charging. The caller ID said *MEPS*. Denny blinked at it, mind fuzzy. Who was MEPS? Outside the porthole, the sun was already up and sparkling over the gorgeous blue ocean.

"Hello?" Denny asked, yawning around the world.

"Up and at 'em, recruit," said an insanely cheerful voice. "I've got some news for you."

"You do?"

"They want you to take another vision test. Can you be here Friday afternoon?"

"What?" Denny scratched the side of his head. "No, wait, is this Master Chief King? This is Denny."

The voice remained cheerful. "Your brother better be out putting in his miles. Tell him noon, sharp, my office, and we'll go to the doctor together."

"I'll tell him," Denny promised.

He changed Steven's ringtone to a Lady Gaga song and turned on the coffeepot.

Steven returned from his run twenty minutes later. When Denny told him about the vision test, he said, "Stop joking around."

"I'm not kidding."

"If you're lying, I'll drown you."

Denny leaned back in his deck chair and tossed him his phone. "Call him back."

Steven walked away down the dock, phone to his ear, toward the *Othello II.* Denny watched him. When Steven came back, he looked a lot less happy than Denny expected.

"What?" Denny asked. "It's good news."

"It's another test!" Steven said.

"So?"

"So, if I failed the last one, I'm going to fail this one, too!"

"You're not color-blind," Denny insisted. "You know it and I know it."

Steven folded his arms and gazed out over the ocean. "We have to dive with Brad and Tristan on Friday."

"I have to dive with Brad and Tristan on Friday," Denny said. "You have to go to Miami. And hey, you can pick up our uniforms on the way back. Win-win."

"You'll need help on Friday," Steven said stubbornly.

"We'll find it," Denny replied. "Come on, I made pancakes."

Steven perked up immediately.

They ate, practiced kicks and katas, and waited for Brad and Tristan. They didn't show up until eight forty-five, and neither looked happy. Denny was about to comment on them being late when he saw the reason why. Ten-year-old Jimmy was with them, a mulish expression on his face.

"His babysitter's sick," Tristan explained. "He has to come out with us today."

Jimmy threatened, "I'm going to throw up over everything. You'll see."

Steven grabbed Brad's camera gear from the back of the van and gave Denny a look that said, *You deal with it.*

Denny decided to accept it all as an unexpected leadership test. "We've got ginger ale. Always good for seasickness."

Jimmy said, "I hate ginger ale."

Brad asked, "Since when?"

"Since I've always hated it," Jimmy replied, eyeing the *Idle* like she was a death trap he was about to be ensnared in.

Tristan muttered, "Drama queen."

Brad's goal for the day was to dive the Gap, a colorful coral canyon four miles southeast of Key Colony Beach, and then a trip to Sombrero Reef.

"I was talking to some people in Key West," he said. "They mentioned a wreck called the *Agana*."

Denny chose his reply carefully. "You must have been talking to some very experienced locals. The *Agana*'s mostly a secret."

Brad didn't back down. "They said she's more interesting than the *Rumney Marsh*."

"More dangerous," Denny said. "Not more interesting. The Coast Guard lists her as a hazard. No reputable dive company would take a tourist out there."

Brad turned away to check on his equipment. Denny waited for him to ask more, to press more, but apparently that was it.

For now at least.

Steven set course and took them out. In the galley, Tristan asked Denny if there was a portable TV on board.

"No," Denny said.

"Everyone has a TV." Jimmy was kicking the leg of the galley table and resolutely not looking out the porthole beside him. "The sitter had a forty-inch screen and HDTV."

"We live a little rougher than that out here," Denny said.

"Any books?" Tristan asked.

Denny grabbed a bottle of water. "There might be a deck of cards in those drawers."

Jimmy said, "I'm too old for Go Fish."

"Play poker," Denny suggested.

"And I'm too young for poker," Jimmy said.

"You're never too young for that," Denny said. "You could be the reigning champ of fourth grade."

Jimmy scowled. "Fifth grade."

"Maybe something other than poker," Tristan suggested.

Denny tried to remember back to games he knew in fifth grade. "How about War? I'll teach you, and then you can beat the pants off Steven."

He taught them the basic rules before it was time to check over the gear. The site didn't have any mooring buoys, so Steven took them carefully over a spot where the anchor would land in sand and not on the fragile reef. Jimmy came out to watch his dad and sister don their gear. He didn't look green, exactly, but he didn't look healthy, either.

"I'm going to hurl," Jimmy threatened.

Denny gave Steven a pointed look. *Your turn.*

Steven scowled.

Brad said, "You'll be fine, Jimmy. Keep your eyes on the horizon and drink that ginger ale."

"But Dad…" Jimmy whined.

"See you later, squirt," Tristan said, and went overboard.

Denny sank happily into the water beside her.

❖

The first vomit appeared five minutes after Steven was left alone with the kid.

"That's just gross," he said, looking at the mess on the galley floor.

Jimmy groaned and curled up on the bench. "It's not my fault."

"I know," Steven said. And he did know seasickness wasn't a

matter of willpower. It was all about the inner ear and equilibrium. He dropped a handful of paper towels on the mess and poured some ginger ale. "Here. Drink this."

Jimmy's face screwed up. "I don't like it."

"And I don't like doing somersaults on a hardwood floor, but sometimes you have to do what you have to do."

"Who makes you do somersaults on a wooden floor?" Jimmy asked, taking the glass but not drinking from it.

"In karate class."

"You do karate? Are you a black belt?"

"Not yet," Steven replied. He couldn't even be sure he'd have one after Saturday. He might freeze up, run out of energy, or just screw up the whole thing altogether. But a bigger problem was the damned vision test on Friday, a totally unexpected development. He couldn't even study for that one. He wished the Navy had just approved the waiver instead of making him go through more torture.

Jimmy sat up. "Will you show me some karate punches?"

"I'll teach you some," Steven said. "If you drink your ginger ale."

Jimmy drank half of it, which was good enough. Steven showed him some stretches, just warming up, and then said, "Stand like this, with your legs turned out and knees bent. This is horse stance."

As far as a cure for seasickness went, karate wasn't it. Jimmy threw up again just fifteen minutes later, and made a more spectacular mess then the first time. He was determined to keep going, though, and so after a brief rest was up and moving again.

"If I learned karate, I could beat up the bullies in my school," Jimmy said.

"You could," Steven acknowledged, "but just because you know how to fight doesn't mean you actually should. Here, punch this way. From the shoulder, not the wrist."

Jimmy copied Steven's move. "Why shouldn't I fight if someone's picking on me?"

"Because karate is a philosophy, too. Defend yourself, but also know when to walk away."

"I'd rather beat up Stanley Delaney," Jimmy said, and tried another punch.

Steven blocked him easily. "Your sister told me she and her boyfriend are pacifists. Glad it doesn't run in the family."

"What boyfriend? She and Matthew broke up." Jimmy stopped to take in a deep breath. "And what's a pacifist?"

"Someone who hates violence. She doesn't have a boyfriend?"

"He dumped her for another girl in their class," Jimmy said. "Am I punching right?"

By the time Brad, Tristan and Denny returned, Jimmy could throw a punch and do three different kinds of blocks.

"I want to take karate classes!" Jimmy said as his dad rested on the portable platform.

"You hate exercise," Brad said.

"It's not exercise," Jimmy said. "Steven says it's a philosophy."

Tristan pulled herself up. "It's still exercise."

She was wearing a green bathing suit today. Steven thought it was the prettiest one of the week. He wondered how Claire would look in that bathing suit, but in his head he heard *you're so cute.* While they ate sandwiches for lunch, Tristan told them all about their trip to Key West and the Mel Fisher museum.

"We had to drag Dad out of there," she said mischievously. "I thought he was going to hide in a corner and stay there overnight."

Brad's cheeks reddened. "Not true."

"Totally true," Tristan said, adding in more details of what they'd seen.

Watching them, Steven realized for the first time how much she tried to encourage and cheer up her father when his mood was bad, which seemed often enough that she had to be constantly on her toes. He remembered what she'd said about her mother leaving.

Maybe Tristan's mother had gotten tired of always trying to bolster her husband. It had to be exhausting.

As they stowed trash in the galley, Steven said to her, "You do a good job with your dad."

"Diving?" she asked.

"And other things."

Tristan rinsed a plastic cup out in the sink. "It's not a lot."

"It seems like a lot," he said.

She gave him a sideways glance, maybe suspecting a tart comment to follow, but Steven kept quiet. He didn't mention anything about Matthew, the missing boyfriend, or ask her why she'd lied to him about it.

Tristan carefully dried the cup. "None of us can control how we feel every day. Emotions just come up, right? Like ocean waves."

"But we can control how we respond to them."

"You and I can," Tristan said. "Imagine if you couldn't walk. If you couldn't dive anymore, or run, or do karate. Imagine someone took that all away from you. Now you need help going to the bathroom and you can't have sex the way you want to and the love of your life decides to leave you. How would you respond to all that?"

She went back on deck, leaving him to think it over.

CHAPTER TWENTY-THREE

Their second spot of the day was Sombrero Reef. Two other dive boats were already on the site when they arrived. The dive and photo shoot with the prop wheelchair went well, though Brad insisted on pushing their underwater time as far as possible again. Steven tried not to lose his temper over that. He was beginning to understand that for Brad, the weightlessness of being underwater must be like having full mobility again. Every moment in the water was a moment away from being dependent on others.

Didn't mean he liked the man, but he supposed he could put up with him for one more day.

And Tristan, too. He'd only have to endure one more day of her pretty face, sharp personality, and sexy bathing suits. Of her secret little smiles, and the way she openly adored her dad, and those stupid astronomy books she lugged on board every day.

She caught him looking at her on the trip back to Fisher Key. "What?" she asked as she rinsed her mask out.

"Nothing," he said, forcing his gaze away.

Back in port, Brad said, "I want to do the *Rumney Marsh* tomorrow and the *Agana* on Friday."

Steven traded glances with Denny.

"We can do the *Rumney Marsh*," Denny said. "But the *Agana*'s off-limits. You want someone to take you out there, it'll have to be someone else."

"I can find someone to do it," Brad said.

"Then you do that," Steven said. "We won't endanger you."

Not that Steven was going to be around Friday anyway, but he hadn't told them that yet.

Brad rolled away in a huff. Tristan followed, shrugging.

Once they were gone, Steven tried to think of someone they could hire to take his place on Friday if Brad changed his mind. The *Othello II* was still in port, so he went over and asked Claire about her plans.

"We should be back at sea by then, if the repairs go well today. If not, I'm still buried under mountains of paperwork."

"You don't know what you're missing. Denny knows all the best spots on the reef."

"I wish I could," Claire replied, sighing.

"You could make it up to me," Steven proposed. "Give me a tour of your top-secret research ship."

Claire laughed. "Top-secret, is it? No one told me. Sure. Come aboard."

The vessel had a galley, crew berthing for eight people, and a cramped marine lab. Bud, another crewman, and a mechanic from the island's biggest boat repair shop were huddled down in engineering, where the big diesel engine wasn't looking good. Steven didn't see Jamie Harrison anywhere. When he asked about him, Claire seemed unconcerned.

"Needed some swimming time," she said. "Being cooped up in port doesn't do him well."

"I thought I saw him with a cut lip last night," Steven said carefully.

Claire shook her head. "Men and their bar fights. I will never understand testosterone."

Steven met more of the crew, and he enjoyed seeing the places where Claire spent her days, but when she gazed at him, he knew she was still seeing a kid. It annoyed him to the bone. On the way back to the *Idle* he thought about calling Jen or Kelsey or Melissa. Just to hang out. Or watch a movie. Nothing more serious than some kissing.

You're only fooling yourself, he thought.

Steven left phone messages with three divers he knew and waited for replies. On the deck of the *Idle,* he called and told his father about the new test. Dad was pleased to hear it.

"You want company on the trip?" Dad asked. "Your mother or me?"

"No," Steven said quickly. He absolutely didn't want to show up at Master Chief King's office with one of his parents in tow. "I'll be good."

Denny emerged from below with a bucket of water and said, once Steven hung up, "I'm going to go take the *Sleuth-hound* out to Franklin Key. You want to call Kelsey or Jen? Bring one along?"

"Shut up."

"Or Melissa Hardy?"

"You're going to look pretty funny taking the black belt test with your mouth crazy-glued shut."

Denny seemed unimpressed.

He called his mom and put her on speakerphone to tell her the news about his test. She gave a little shriek of delight and said, "I knew they'd see their mistake!"

"They're not saying they made a mistake. It just means I might not pass again," Steven warned.

She scoffed. "You'll do fine."

"We'll see."

"What are you boys doing for the rest of the day?"

"I'm going swimming," Steven said. A good long swim around the key would be great for his stress level and for physical fitness. "Denny's going to take his boat out before she dies of neglect—"

Denny started waving his hands frantically. Steven had no idea what he was doing. Denny accidentally knocked over the bucket he'd brought up, and soapy water spilled over the deck.

"—and I think that would be nice," Mom was saying over the clatter. "We can meet you there in a half hour. What's that noise?"

"Denny's being a klutz," Steven said, distracted. "What did you say?"

"Oh, I said it would be nice to give Aunt Riza a ride around the island," Mom repeated. "We'll be there in a half hour."

Steven hung up. Denny gave him a murderous glower.

"I didn't suggest it," Steven said. "It's not my fault!"

"I already asked Brian to come," Denny said scathingly. "I can't have him, Aunt Riza, and Mom on the same boat."

"Why not?"

"Because she hates gays!"

"She doesn't hate gays," Steven said. "She just hates finding out her nephew is gay by catching him making out on the sofa with another guy."

"She thinks it's a phase I'm going to outgrow."

"So what?" Steven asked. "Twenty years from now, you'll still be gay. That'll show her."

"I'm not disinviting him."

"Maybe she'll get to know him better and let you invite him to the party."

Denny looked ridiculously unhappy. "It's going to be a disaster," he predicted. "And you're coming along, since you started it."

"I started what?" Steven demanded.

"And whatever you do, don't mention the party," Denny said. "Don't let them talk about it at all."

Steven sighed. "You're so weird."

Denny called Brian and warned him that Aunt Riza was coming. Steven called Mom and told her Brian would be there, too. Thirty minutes later they all met up at the house, where the roofers had made some progress but were packing up for the day. Mom and Aunt Riza both wore khaki shorts, sensible sandals, and flowered blouses. Aunt Riza didn't look any happier than Denny.

Brian, however, was perfectly polite. "Nice to see you again, Mrs. Anderson."

"You, too, Brian," Mom said. "This is my sister, Riza Valencia. You weren't formally introduced."

"Mrs. Valencia," Brian said, and offered his hand.

Gingerly she took it. "It's nice to meet you."

Steven almost commented that it wasn't the first time they'd met, but Denny picked up the cooler Brian had brought and shoved it into Steven's hands. "Let's go before we run out of daylight."

The cooler was full of food, which again proved how smart Brian was. Steven crammed a chicken salad sandwich into his mouth as Denny steered the *Sleuth-hound* across the water. Steven realized, too late, that Brian and Denny had been planning some alone time on the beach—which was exactly the kind of information Steven didn't need to know. He didn't care at all that Denny was gay, but he didn't want to picture him getting anything on with another guy. That was just…well, weird. Mostly because he found nothing at all alluring about kissing a guy with his stubble and hair and the same male junk that Steven himself had.

"So, Brian," Mom said. "Are you getting ready for your move to Boston? Ree, Brian's going to MIT. He's very smart."

Brian looked uncomfortable. "The plans are kind of flexible right now."

Steven remembered Denny saying something about that. It was kind of funny that Steven and Brian and even Eddie were all in approximately the same place, Limbo, even if they'd arrived there in different ways. Funny in a frustrating, annoying, futile way that Steven didn't want to dwell on. Uncertainty had never been one of his favorite things.

Aunt Riza asked, "What are you going to study?"

"History," Brian said. "I know everyone goes there for engineering and science, but I'm more of a liberal arts kind of person."

"Are you liberal?" Aunt Riza asked.

"Let's not talk politics," Mom said.

Aunt Riza lifted her chin. "You should go into the military like my nephews. No liberals there."

Steven didn't correct her on the political leanings of U.S. soldiers and sailors. But he didn't think Brian would last more than one day in any military. Not because he was gay or soft or anything but because he didn't have the mindset. He said, "It's not for everyone. Denny's been a geek about the Coast Guard since we were ten. I think he'd pay them to let him go, if he had to."

Brian cocked his head. "You think he's going to like it at the academy?"

Steven had read the material the parents' association had sent to Mom and Dad—what swabs should bring, and how they would have very little time to call home, and how the best thing parents could do was to be encouraging and supportive. Maybe for some cadets it was all going to be a culture shock. Denny was going to love it. He'd probably end up first in his class.

But he was also probably going to be homesick, too. Neither Steven nor Denny had ever spent much time away from Fisher Key. And there was the whole gay thing, too. It would only take one homophobic classmate or by-the-books instructor to ruin things in New London, or at least make them very difficult for Denny to bear.

"Denny will make us very proud," Mom said, holding her hair so that it didn't whip in the breeze. "Steven, you, too."

He wasn't so sure about that anymore. Not if he didn't get into BUD/S.

Denny brought the boat into the shallows around Franklin Key and anchored her. They all waded ashore, Brian carrying the cooler and Denny carrying a blanket, with Steven helping Mom and Aunt

Riza. The beach here wasn't very big, but a scenic hiking path led through the interior to the old quarry.

Denny said, "I'm going to show Brian around."

"Show us, too," Mom said. "I haven't been to the quarry in years."

Denny shot Steven a pointed look. Steven thought about letting him squirm, but took pity.

"I'll show you, Mom," he said.

Mom turned to Brian. "Don't you want to see it?"

"I'll show him later," Denny said, through gritted teeth.

For a moment, Mom seemed perplexed. Then she said, "Oh! Yes. Later."

They left Brian and Denny on the beach. Aunt Riza looked over her shoulder with a frown, suspecting something amiss, but Steven distracted her by pointing out the mahogany and ironwood trees that were native to the keys. The quarry wasn't so much a hole in the ground as a slow rise of the ancient reef around them. Soon they were flanked by the eight-foot walls, which had once been far underwater but were now mossy and green with plant growth.

"What did they do with the rock they took away?" Aunt Riza asked.

"Built bridges and stuff," Steven replied. "Causeways to connect the keys. There's a plaque over here."

Aunt Riza squinted at something beyond Steven's shoulder. "Something's wrong with those trees."

He turned, expected to just see some had toppled in storms, but she was right—something had smashed right through a cluster of joewoods above the coral wall. Steven hiked up to find out more. Moments later, he was staring down at a battered metal object the size of a motorcycle sitting in a crater.

"What did you find?" Mom called up.

Steven grinned. "NASA's missing satellite!"

CHAPTER TWENTY-FOUR

A blanket, the ocean, and Brian—Denny really couldn't ask for more. He'd be ecstatic if only his mother and aunt weren't nearby and likely to interrupt any minute.

"Come on, relax," Brian said, stroking his arm. They were sitting on the blanket together, the cooler open near their legs, their sandwiches and drinks barely touched. "You're going to give yourself a stroke."

Denny replied, "I didn't want her to come along. Any of them. This was just supposed to be us."

"Stuff happens," Brian said. "How far is the quarry?"

"Ten minutes from here."

"So we've got some time."

"Not enough," Denny replied.

Brian's hands slid lower. "We'll just have to work fast."

"We can't," Denny said, laughing, squirming away. "If my mom comes back and we're in the middle of anything, I'll die of embarrassment."

Brian eyed the ocean speculatively. "Then we'd better go swimming."

They waded into the water but Denny wouldn't exactly call it swimming—there was kissing and groping, sun glinting off water, the warm waves lifting and dropping them, pushing and pulling. Denny's hands roamed over Brian in a way that he'd only dreamed about. He'd never thought he could have this, not before the academy and certainly not while there.

"You are the handsomest guy on this island," Brian murmured. "I don't think I've told you that enough."

Denny grinned as he tasted Brian's lips and rubbed his broad, smooth back. "No, I think that's you."

Brian tugged him into a wave. "We'll have to wrestle over it."

Denny let the water wash over him. He loved doing this with Brian. He loved the sky and sun above them, the wind on his neck, the rising and falling ocean, the boy in his arms. But soon it would be over—there'd be no summer waves in New London, nobody to hold and kiss, probably not even anyone to confide in. Just secrets and furtive glances and the danger of being discharged if anyone found out.

"Hey, where'd you go?" Brian asked suddenly, his hand on Denny's face.

Denny blinked at him. "What? I'm right here."

"You're a thousand miles away," Brian complained.

"No, I'm not," Denny promised. He surged forward on a wave, landed atop Brian, and pulled him into his arms. "Right here for three more weeks."

They kissed again, hands going lower, skin rubbing against skin. Just as Denny thought maybe tonight he'd reach a milestone— thank goodness, finally!—Steven burst out of the trees.

"Call the Coast Guard!" he said, all excited. "We found it!"

Denny wanted to drown himself.

If he thought his evening had been ruined before, it was ruined all over again when the Coast Guard showed up to investigate Steven's claim. The Navy arrived as well. Mom and Aunt Riza took great delight in it all. Steven strutted around, proud as anything, even though it had been Denny's idea to come out to Franklin Key in the first place.

"Good job," said a Navy lieutenant who'd come ashore.

"Just lucky," Steven said modestly. "Is that all of it?"

The lieutenant watched several seamen lift the object. Other sailors were beating through the bushes, looking for more parts. "I guess so. They'll examine it back in the lab."

Denny was bored by the whole thing. He waited impatiently until it was time to return to Fisher Key, by which time the sun had gone down and stars were smattering across the sky. Dad was waiting at the pier, sitting on the hood of his patrol car with some buckets of fried chicken.

"I hear a celebration is in order," he said.

Brian pulled Denny aside. "I'd love to stay, but I've got to go check on Mom."

"Okay," Denny said. "Call me."

It was dark, and Aunt Riza was helping Mom light some citronella to keep the bugs away. Denny risked a quick kiss. Brian's mouth was warm and salty and he had a sappy grin on his face.

I think I love you, Denny almost said, but caught himself.

"See you later," Brian said, and when he drove away it was like Denny had to let a part of himself drive away as well.

When he returned to the picnic bench, Steven was already on his second piece of chicken.

"There should be a reward," he said. "I'll split it with you, Aunt Riza."

She waved her hand with a smile. "Anyone could have found it."

This dinner was a lot more relaxed than the last one. Denny was glad that Aunt Riza hadn't done anything to make Brian uncomfortable. Mom, too, had been very casual and cool about the whole thing. He wondered how cool she would be if he said, "By the way, I think I'm in love with this guy." Not that he would say it. Not that it could be true. Still, Denny wanted to get Brian back into the ocean as soon as possible. Maybe they could go skinny-dipping—

"By Saturday," Dad was saying, and Denny stopped zoning out on him.

"Huh?" Denny asked.

"The roof should be fixed by Saturday," Dad was saying. "Another week to get the carpeting and painting all set. Then we can all move back in."

"You can pick out the color you want for your walls," Mom said.

Steven bit into his chicken and shrugged. Denny didn't think he himself should pick the colors, not when he was going to be away for most of every year until he graduated from the academy.

"You pick, Mom," Denny said. "Whatever you like."

Mom pursed her lips thoughtfully. "I always wanted purple."

"With a yellow accent wall," Dad added.

Steven coughed around his chicken. "You don't even know what an accent wall is, Dad!"

"I watch HGTV in the lunchroom at the station," Dad said. "It's very educational."

Mom's phone rang with a call from the local newspaper, asking about the satellite find. Denny left her, Aunt Riza, and Steven to tell the tale. He helped Dad throw away the remains of dinner and was a little surprised when Dad asked, "How are things going with Brad Flaherty?"

"Okay, I guess," Denny said.

"I heard he was up at Darla Stewart's shop this afternoon, asking about the *Agana*."

Denny's pulse quickened. "What did they tell him?"

"The same thing they tell every overambitious tourist. It's not open to the public. He's going to have to look hard for someone who's going to take him, and it's not because of that wheelchair."

Denny said, "He asked us to take him Friday. We said no. I don't care if he fires us."

Dad patted his shoulder. "If he fires you, look on the bright side. You can rest up and get ready for your test. Or spend Friday with Brian."

Okay, that was definitely a good idea. With Steven away, Denny would have the *Idle* all to himself. He could take Brian out for an entire day's sail. They could go find a private beach, get suntan oil all over each other…

"I can see you making plans already," Dad said.

Denny blushed and turned away.

He was so excited about the new plan that he was surprised, later, when he told Steven about Brad and Steven got annoyed.

"We've told him he's not ready," Steven said. "It's too dangerous."

They were walking back to the marina from their house. It was a short trip along an old dirt path. The ocean lapped quietly just a few feet away. The night was warm and fragrant, quiet but for some lights and laughter from some offshore boats.

Denny replied, "Maybe he doesn't think he should listen to a couple of eighteen-year-olds."

"Smartest eighteen-year-olds on this island," Steven grumbled.

As they approached the marina, they saw a taxi pull into the parking lot. Claire stepped out, her face tight and angry, and stalked toward the *Othello II*. Harrison paid the driver and followed her closely, saying something, but they were too far away to be heard clearly.

"She doesn't look happy," Denny observed.

"Guy's a jerk, I told you," Steven said.

Harrison caught Claire's arm and pulled her to a stop. She spun on him, her free hand raised in a slap. He caught it and pushed her backward so hard she staggered on her heels.

Steven started to run, but he was too late.

Harrison punched Claire in the face. She fell to the pier and didn't get up.

CHAPTER TWENTY-FIVE

Steven sprinted down the dock. Harrison saw him coming and warned, "Stay out of this, kid—" but Steven didn't bother with conversation. He barreled right into Harrison, trying to knock him flat.

But Harrison wasn't easy to overpower. He went down, but took Steven with him. They rolled close to the dock's edge, grappling, swearing at each other. Steven brought his knee up hard. Harrison twisted and Steven's knee hit the dock instead with a bright flare of pain. Harrison tried to land a kidney punch. Steven twisted, spat in Harrison's face, and got his arm against the other man's windpipe.

"Easy to hit a girl," Steven snarled. "Harder to hit me."

Harrison's thumbs came up, aiming for Steven's eyes. Steven had to lift his arm away to block, and Harrison bucked him off. Steven would have tumbled into the water except for Denny, who grabbed him by the shoulder and hauled him back. Harrison's friend Bud, along with another man from the crew, grabbed him and pinned him into place.

"Let me go!" Harrison was yelling. "Goddamned kid has no business—"

Steven almost lunged for him again, but Denny's grip was firm. "Quit it," Denny growled.

Boaters had gathered on their top decks or on the dock to watch the spectacle. Claire, nearly forgotten by everyone, was sitting up with one hand pressed to her jaw. She looked dazed and teary-eyed, her blouse disheveled.

"Let me help her," Steven said to Denny.

Denny let him go. Steven helped Claire up, asking, "Are you okay? Did he break it?"

She shook her head angrily but didn't say anything.

Bud turned around. "You're fired, Harrison. You'll never work for this company again, or any company if I have a say in it."

Harrison glared at him. "Me? I didn't do anything!"

"He punched her," Denny said. He looked as angry as Steven felt, but not as violent.

"You want to press charges?" Bud asked Claire.

Claire shook her head again. "I want him gone."

Steven was tempted to call Dad anyway. That way they'd have a record of it in case there was trouble later. But Bud and his men simply walked Harrison up to the parking lot while a crew member packed his things. Claire went aboard the *Othello II* without a thank you or anything else to Steven. He guessed she felt embarrassed, or furious, or both.

"My, that was unexpected," said a man behind Steven. "Are you all right, son?"

"I'm fine," Steven said, but that was a lie. His knee was throbbing. He blinked past the pain to focus on the retired NASA worker he'd met at the Li'l Conch Café. His wife was a few feet behind him, on the deck of a small cabin cruiser. It took a moment for Steven to remember their names—Ed and Irma. He hadn't realized they were boaters.

"I'm fine," Steven said, and it was mostly true.

"Your lip is bleeding," Ed said. "Irma, get the kit."

Steven felt his mouth. His fingers came away red. "It's nothing, really," he said, because he'd had worse in sparring.

"Come over here and I'll get you some ice," Irma said. "You don't want a big fat lip in the morning."

Denny looked amused. "It might improve his looks."

Ed did a double take between them. "Twins, eh? I knew some twins once. Back in Iowa City. Don't tell Irma."

"Heard that," she called back.

Steven really didn't need to be mother-henned, but Irma's attention was sweet and from the deck of their boat he could keep an eye on Harrison, who was still up in the parking lot. Ed said, "Heard on the radio there was some excitement at Bardet Key. They found our satellite, huh?"

"Steven found it," Denny said.

"It was just good luck," Steven replied.

"All of it?" Irma asked, dabbing Steven's lip with an antiseptic wipe. "Or just some pieces?"

Steven replied, "It looked intact."

"You can't always tell," Ed said sagely. "What's the story with that fellow and the fight?"

A cab pulled into the parking lot. Steven watched closely as Harrison got into it. "He's just a jerk."

"No man should ever hit a woman," Irma said. "I'd shoot him square between the eyes."

Denny asked, curiously, "Do you have a gun on board, ma'am?"

She winked at him. "Two of them. But don't tell Ed. He only thinks there's one."

"I heard that," Ed said, and kissed her.

Steven watched the cab pull away. He had the heavy, disconcerting feeling that it wasn't the last they'd see of Harrison. Trouble like him had a habit of showing up again when you least expected it.

❖

The next morning, Steven's knee was swollen and achy and he decided it might be better to skip his morning run.

"How about you go see the doctor?" Denny asked.

"How about you don't worry about it," Steven replied.

"In forty-eight hours we'll be taking the black belt test. What if it's not healed?"

"It'll be fine," Steven said.

They were on deck, practicing some punches, when Claire walked over. She was wearing oversized sunglasses and the side of her face was bruised.

"About last night," she said, her Irish accent stronger than ever. "I wanted to apologize for getting you involved."

"It wasn't your fault," Steven said, stopping the kata. He swung down to the dock but didn't try to get too close to her. "He deserved what he got."

Denny leaned over the railing. "He deserved worse."

Her gaze went past them both to a pair of seagulls squawking on a post. "He made a proposition. Not a romantic one—a business one. Which I disagreed with on ethical grounds. And so he was angry."

Steven wanted to soothe the lost sound in her voice. To be truthful, he wanted to hold her and tell her that he'd protect her forever. "Being angry doesn't give him the right to hit you."

"On that we agree," Claire said. "Anyway, this isn't the first job he's been fired from and it won't be the last. He's gone now. Just in time, too—our sister ship recovered the satellite yesterday."

Denny said, "Actually, Steven found it."

Her mouth quirked. "Oh, that was you? They said it was a kid and his mom."

Steven rolled his eyes. "Not a kid."

Claire smiled fully now. "Well done. But it means the job is over. We're moving the boat over to a marine yard to finish repairs on the engine and most of us are flying back to Virginia. Which is a shame—I like your little island."

Denny said, "We like it, too."

"Good luck with the Coast Guard, Denny. And Steven, you too with the SEALS. I know you'll both be wonderful."

She stepped close to Steven and kissed his right cheek. Her soft lips smelled like strawberry gloss. "Thanks for last night," she murmured.

Steven watched her retreat down the dock. He'd probably never see her again.

"Come on, Romeo," Denny said. "Brad and Tristan will be here in a half hour, and we have to tell them that you won't be here tomorrow."

CHAPTER TWENTY-SIX

Y ou're all smiley this morning," Mom said over breakfast.
    "Am I?" Brian asked, playing innocent. He wasn't about
to tell her he and Denny had been exchanging sappy text messages
for half the night. Denny thought maybe they'd have the *Idle* to
themselves tomorrow. If so, they might go out to a private beach.
And things would progress from there, in whatever way felt best for
both of them...

    "And now you're zoning out on me," Mom complained, but
her eyes were soft and fond. "I know this college thing has been
hard. It's good to see you relax."

    "It's all been harder on you," he said, truthfully. "College and
Henrik and the money and everything."

    Her hand was steady on her orange juice glass. "Day by day.
That's the trick, right?"

    He wished she looked a little more confident when she said it,
but at least the sentiment sounded right. Day by day indeed.

    Come midmorning, he was tired of hanging around the hotel.
Duma Key was only going to last him another hundred pages, so
he drove over to the Bookmine to look through the shelves for
something new to read. Mrs. Anderson was at the front counter,
taping up a huge box of books.

    "Hi, Brian," she said. "Can I ask you to help me move this?
Sean's out today. It goes right there, that corner."

"Sure," he said. The box wasn't too heavy at all. "How's your morning? No news crews when you opened?"

She laughed. "Sadly enough, finding a multimillion-dollar piece of equipment didn't get us on the morning news."

"I guess that's good. I'm not a big fan of reporters sticking their microphones in my face."

"Me neither," she said.

The store around them was empty, the air quiet except for some classical music playing on the radio. Mrs. Anderson gazed at him frankly and said, "I wanted to thank you for all you're doing for Denny. It means a lot to us, to see him happy for a change."

"He's not usually happy?" Brian asked, feeling a pang.

"I can't say that, but he's always been…maybe 'lonely' is the word," Mrs. Anderson said. "He was afraid to tell us for so long. When you keep a secret like that, it weighs you down. And of course he wouldn't let himself date or have fun. So, a boyfriend is a good thing."

Brian blushed. He hadn't been thinking of himself as Denny's boyfriend, but he guessed they were at that stage by now.

Mrs. Anderson patted his hand. "And I wanted to thank you for being understanding about Denny's going away party. My sister is a very wonderful person, but too rigid in her thinking. I'm working on her, though. Give me some more time, and I think I can get her to come around. Eventually."

Brian thought back to his and Denny's dinner date down in Marathon. *Family party*, Denny had said. Not *my going away party*. Carefully he said, "In the meantime, it's best if I don't come."

Her phone rang. She said, warmly, "Thanks for understanding," and turned to answer it.

He left without buying anything. The short drive back to the hotel was made with fingers clenched on the steering wheel. He parked and pulled out his phone and typed a message: *I wasn't even invited to your stupid party, was I?*

But Denny was out at sea, of course. He wouldn't be able to answer. Brian deleted it. He felt adrift with anger and hurt, with nothing to do about it until Denny came back to shore.

Nothing except call Sean.

❖

"I don't understand why people sink perfectly good ships," Tristan remarked as they headed out toward the site of the *Rumney Marsh*.

"Because they can," Brad said.

"Because they can help replace natural reef that we've destroyed," Denny said. "A nice new home for fish and other marine life that need it."

They moored to an underwater buoy. Although Steven's knee ached, he made the first dive with Brad and Tristan. The water was crystal clear and perfect for diving. It took a few minutes for the *Rumney Marsh* to come into view. She was a big ship, almost two hundred feet long. During her days at sea she'd been a research vessel, investigating lightning strikes, but now the entire wreck served as an enormous submerged home for angelfish, tarpon, and a dozen other types of fish.

The wreck was so deep they couldn't spend a lot of time on the bottom. Most of it was spent getting the prop wheelchair into position without damaging any marine growth. They ascended as scheduled, took a break, computed time for the next dive, and descended again. The second dive was shorter, thanks to the nitrogen already built up in their blood, and Brad spent most of it taking photos.

When Brad started to descend below eighty feet, Steven tapped his dive computer meaningfully. Going down farther meant shaving off more minutes.

Brad looked annoyed behind his mask, but Steven tapped the gauge again and got a reluctant nod.

"I think that's my favorite spot yet," Tristan said while they ate lunch. "We should come back here tomorrow."

"Tomorrow I want to do the *Agana*," Brad replied.

Steven gave Denny a pointed look.

Denny said, "We told you. We don't take anyone there."

"It's because I'm paralyzed, isn't it?" Brad demanded. His face was turning red. "It's about the damned wheelchair."

Denny said, "No, it's because it's dangerous."

Tristan said, quietly, "We can go somewhere else—back to the Gap, or Thunder Shoals—"

"I can find someone else," Brad threatened. "There's plenty of master divers on this island."

"And they're all going to say no," Steven countered. He didn't tell Brad they already knew about his visit to Darla Stewart. "No one wants that kind of liability."

"So now I'm a liability," Brad said snippishly.

Steven didn't answer. He didn't think Brad would listen to reason and he wasn't willing to put more effort into it. He left Denny to deal with them and climbed up to the wheelhouse. Tristan came up a short time later, her face somber.

"He sets his heart on things and gets frustrated when he can't have them," she said.

"Join the club," Steven said, pretending to be intensely interested in the weather report.

"It's easy for you," Tristan retorted. "I bet you've never had anyone say no to you in your entire life."

"Which shows how much you don't know about me," Steven said hotly.

She turned her head to the horizon. "This is the only trip he can afford this year. For the next few years, unless he wins the lottery. His job, the divorce, my college—I get it, you don't want to hear our problems. But you live here all the time, so you take it for granted. But we can't."

"That's not a good reason to risk his life. Or yours."

She stalked away, muttering under her breath.

Brad was mad, but not mad enough to cancel the afternoon's trip to Sombrero Reef again. As they approached the site, Steven was surprised to see the Navy ship and the *Othello I* in the area.

"I bet they're still missing a piece or two," he said.

Denny said, "You're not going to get lucky twice. Besides, I'm going down this trip."

"We could trade," Steven suggested.

"Forget it," Denny said.

The snorkeling went well enough, though Brad was still tight-lipped and sulking about the *Agana* when they came back. In fact, he sulked all the way back to Fisher Key, and sulked while Denny and Steven helped him ashore. Ed and Irma's boat was gone from its slip, but another familiar boat had tied up in its slot.

"Oh, no," Steven muttered.

"Ahoy!" said Larry Gold, tanned and muscular in his tight T-shirt. He came striding down the dock. "You're Brad Flaherty, right? My bad. I've been stuck in Pensacola all week with a bad engine, and I lost my phone the week before that. Otherwise I would never have left you dangling in the wind."

Steven thought that was a lot of excuses, but Brad shook Larry's hand and Larry beamed as if they were all old friends. There was a saying around the marina: *Never trust Larry with your wallet or your wife.* Being a good diver didn't make him a good person.

"Nice of you boys to take care of my client," he said to Denny and Steven. "Everyone says you can count on the Andersons."

"That's right," Steven said, lifting one of Brad's camera cases. "We've been working all week."

Denny added, "A lot of good diving."

"I'm sure, I'm sure," Larry said heartily. "But I bet I know a few sweet spots these boys haven't figured out yet."

Brad gave him a considering look. "What about the *Agana*?"

Larry scratched the side of his head. "Great spot. I take all my best divers there."

Steven put down the camera case forcefully. "He doesn't have the experience, Larry."

"It's too dangerous for either of them," Denny put in.

Tristan watched carefully but said nothing, her hand on her father's shoulder.

"I think I'm a better judge of that than you are, boys," Larry said. "I've been diving since you were still in diapers."

Denny opened his mouth as if to argue. Steven beat him to it, saying, "You could get them killed."

Larry's smile didn't dim a single bit. "Ain't never gotten anyone killed yet, and I'm not about to start now. Come on, Brad, let's talk details."

Brad rolled off with him. Steven watched in disbelief, trying to marshal up more arguments, but Tristan shrugged at them and followed her father, and what was Steven supposed to do about it, anyway? They weren't doing anything against the law.

Denny said, "I can't believe he's going to take him."

Steven said, "Not our problem."

"But they're not ready—"

"Not our problem," Steven repeated. "You can take the *Idle* out with Brian while I'm up in Miami."

Denny appeared marginally cheered up by that, although he kept throwing worried glances toward Larry's boat. He and Steven cleaned and stowed their gear, then got the *Idle* shipshape. Denny tried to reach Brian but got no answer. Steven's phone beeped with several text messages that had accumulated during the day, including Kelsey and Jennifer and Melissa Hardy. He wanted to pitch the phone right into the ocean.

"Yes, it's so hard being popular," Denny said after Steven complained.

"I'm not popular. I'm being stalked."

Denny remained entirely unsympathetic.

"I'm starving," Steven said. "Let's go eat."

"Do you really think you can risk an appearance in public?" Denny asked.

"Do you really want me to drown you?" Steven replied.

CHAPTER TWENTY-SEVEN

Denny was surprised Brian hadn't sent him any messages during the day. They'd been awake until past midnight, trading texts, and he was feeling very hopeful about the big countdown calendar in his head. Eighteen days left. No more ferrying Brad and Tristan on the *Idle*. Once he got past the black belt test on Saturday, and Aunt Riza's party on Sunday, he and Brian would have two weeks together. Two weeks of boat trips and beach blankets and more fun in the surf, if Denny had anything to say about it.

He tried texting Brian from the marina, but nothing came back. He hoped that didn't mean bad news—maybe MIT had told him he definitely couldn't come, or Brian's mom had taken a mental turn for the worse.

Steven drove them over to the Li'l Conch Café. The parking lot was mostly empty—too late for lunch, too early for dinner. When Denny walked in, he saw a few tourists sitting by the green mermaid statue, some kids from the high school at the counter, and Brian and Sean in a booth against the wall.

Brian and Sean.

Which explained why Brian hadn't called him back.

Denny stopped so abruptly that Steven ran into him.

"What?" Steven asked, annoyed, and then, "Oh."

Denny couldn't move. Not that he distrusted Brian. Absolutely not. But there was his best friend and his sort-of boyfriend, sitting together and smiling, and Brian hadn't tried to reach him all day, hadn't called him back, and what was Denny supposed to think?

"Oh" just about summed it up.

Brian looked their way, saw Denny, and grimaced. Honest-to-goodness grimaced, as if Denny's very existence in the world was a physical pain. Like a kidney stone, which Denny's dad had suffered from for a whole week once. That look was nothing Denny wanted to ever see on someone he hoped to spend a lot of time with.

Louanne Garrity was standing behind the counter, thumbing something into her phone. "Sit yourselves down," she called out.

Brian turned back to Sean, deliberately dismissing Denny. Sean glanced over, saw who was in the doorway, and raised his hand in a halfhearted wave.

"Hey," he called out.

Not a "come join us" hey or a "good to see you" hey but just hey, as if they were all casual acquaintances who'd just happened to cross paths.

"Hi," Denny said in return, though his tongue felt kind of weird and he wasn't sure it came out loud enough to be heard.

Behind him, Steven asked, "Do you want to go somewhere else?"

"Of course not," Denny said, because there was no need to be silly about it. He walked to a booth that was the exact farthest point from Brian and slid onto the blue vinyl bench with his back toward him. Although he knew the menu by heart, he grabbed one of the laminated lists from where it was clipped to the napkins and pretended to read every word.

Steven sat down opposite him. "We can go get pizza at Sal's."

"I want to eat here," Denny said flatly.

"Okay." Steven didn't sound convinced. "I'm just offering."

The satellite radio system started playing something romantic and sappy, just to torture Denny. He let a moment pass while Steven fiddled on his phone, and asked, "What are they doing now?"

"Really?" Steven asked. "We're going to play this game?"

"Shut up and tell me."

"They're kissing," Steven said.

Denny almost whipped around in shock, but he didn't. "Liar."

"Of course I'm lying. They're just sitting there, eating. Like we're going to do, or I'll die of starvation," Steven said.

Louanne came over with some biscuits and took their orders. The biscuits were a little burnt and Louanne a little brusque; Denny figured she was having a bad day. If she noticed any awkwardness going on between her customers, she didn't say anything. Denny didn't have the excuse of the menu anymore so he pulled out his own phone. No one had sent him any messages or e-mail. He tapped his favorite site about the Coast Guard Academy but all the words seemed too small, completely unreadable.

He listened hard, trying to figure out what Sean and Brian were talking about, but the romantic music was too loud.

"What are they doing now?"

"I'm going to shoot you with a flare gun," Steven said. "Stop torturing yourself."

"It's not torture. It's information."

"Get your information the old-fashioned way and go talk to them," Steven suggested.

Denny insisted, "They should come over here."

"You are just like a twelve-year-old girl," Steven said. "Last night you were frisky in the surf and tonight you think he's cheating on you?"

"We weren't frisky," Denny replied. But of course they were. He felt a pang at how nice it had been to feel Brian's hands and taste his lips and now they were like strangers, and he didn't know why.

The bell rang behind him, signifying someone leaving or entering. Steven's gaze went past Denny's shoulder and he blanched.

"Oh, man," he said. "Ambushed."

Denny had to turn around to see. Kelsey, Jennifer, and Melissa had come in, all of them shiny and pretty, a trio of best friends forever. They took a round table in the middle of the room and didn't cast a single gaze toward Steven. Melissa tossed her blond hair and Jennifer adjusted her red miniskirt and Kelsey applied a new layer of pink gloss. When Louanne went to them with a big smile, it was just like the Three Musketeers meeting up with d'Artagnan. Next there'd be a revolution, and Denny figured there'd be two Anderson heads on the chopping block.

"She called them, I know she did," Steven muttered. "You can't trust anyone these days."

Denny's gaze slid by the girls to Brian, who was gazing right back at him. Still with that unhappy, pained look. Denny turned right back around, heart pounding.

"I say we run for our lives," Steven said. "Right out the back door."

But he didn't make a move, and neither did Denny. The romantic song segued into something even sappier. Louanne served drinks to Melissa, Kelsey, and Jennifer before she brought Steven and Denny's without a smile.

Denny tasted his. "I think she spiked it with diet."

Steven pushed his glass away. "We're lucky if they're not poisoned."

"I get that you're a jerk, but what did I do?"

"I'm not a jerk," Steven protested. "I took a vow."

"And ignored everyone's messages," Denny pointed out.

Steven picked up his phone and stared into the screen. "I'm just going to pretend I'm somewhere else now."

Denny wished he could do the same. Instead, he was hyperaware of Brian staring at the back of his head. Like laser beams boring into his skull. When he couldn't stand it anymore he stood up.

"Where are you going?" Steven said sharply.

"Bathroom."

"If you crawl out the window, I'll kill you."

"You'd have to catch me first," Denny retorted.

The bathroom window was large enough, sure, but he wasn't in there to escape. He splashed cold water on his face and searched his reflection for signs of guilt. Brian was the one who should feel guilty. Not returning messages, having dinner behind his back... Denny tried to muster enough indignation to return to the table. When he emerged, shoulders squared, Sean was waiting for him in the narrow hallway.

"I thought maybe you drowned in there," Sean said.

"No," Denny said awkwardly. "Didn't drown."

"So it's none of my business, I know," Sean went on, "but you need to go in there and apologize and maybe he'll listen. I mean, not right in there, because he kind of left, but I asked him to wait in the parking lot—"

Denny cut him off. "What am I apologizing for?"

Sean gave him an incredulous look. "Hello? The party that you didn't invite him to? I'd be mad, too."

"The party..." Denny groaned. "Aunt Riza."

"Your mom let it slip."

"I didn't mean to," Denny said, but it sounded lame to his own ears. Didn't mean to keep the news from Brian? Didn't mean to mislead him? He'd done Brian wrong and they both knew it.

Sean punched him lightly in the arm. "Go grovel, champ."

❖

Brian knew Fisher Key was small—you could walk the island from north to south in an hour—but it was rotten luck Denny had walked right into the place where he and Sean were having dinner. Then again, there weren't that many restaurants on the island, and maybe he'd hoped Denny would find them there.

Standing in the parking lot as the sun dipped in the west, he tried not to think too hard about the flash of hurt that had crossed Denny's face. The quick, pained flinch of someone who thought he'd been betrayed. Not that Sean and Brian were doing anything wrong, really. Commiseration was not a crime. Brian needed advice on handling Denny and this whole party thing, and Sean was the best source of information.

"He's really upset," Sean had said, when Denny and Steven sat in the far booth.

"How can you tell?"

"He sits up straighter when he's hiding something," Sean said, dipping his very last French fry into a pool of ketchup. "Go talk to him."

Brian felt a little glow of satisfaction that Denny was hurt. He deserved it. At the same time, it caused a twisty feeling in Brian's gut, and the onion rings on his plate turned completely unappealing. He insisted, "He should come over here."

"He won't." Sean sighed. "You really want to play games? You waiting for him, him waiting for you? I mean, maybe it feels righteous or something, but I think it's just a waste of time. Get it over with, like ripping off a bandage."

Brian wasn't convinced. He remained in his seat and watched as Steven's sort-of girlfriend Kelsey came in with two of her friends. Denny didn't turn around. Sean's sister Louanne was overly friendly with the girls but gave Denny and Steven curt service. Brian couldn't bring himself to care.

When Denny went to the bathroom, Brian decided it was time to leave.

"Thanks for listening," he said, pulling out enough money for both of their tabs. "I've got to go."

Sean rolled his eyes. "Wait in the parking lot, okay? Don't leave. I'll get him out there."

"How?"

"Trust me. I am wise in the ways of Andersons."

Standing in the crushed-shell side lot, hands in his pockets, Brian tried to figure out what Denny was going to say, and what he'd say in return. It was like writing a movie script in his head.

Denny would probably say something like, "My aunt's embarrassed about me."

Brian would reply, "That doesn't mean you can hurt other people."

Denny would say, "I didn't mean to hurt you."

And Brian would say, "Someone always gets hurt when you lie."

He was so busy rehearsing lines that he almost missed Denny's footsteps behind him. He turned as Denny stopped a few feet away. Denny had a stricken look on his face, equal parts ashamed and contrite.

"I'm sorry," he said, before Brian could even say anything. "I shouldn't have lied about it. That was a crappy thing to do."

Brian took a deep breath. "Yeah. It was."

Denny's gaze remained steady. He didn't seem to notice the cars whizzing by on the Overseas Highways nearby, or the noisy tourists piling out of a jeep that had just parked, or the hum as the neon lights flickered on in the Li'l Conch's large rooftop sign.

"I don't know how to do it yet," Denny said. "How you balance what you want and your family wants, or what you owe them and what you owe people you love."

Brian felt sucker-punched.

"You think you love me?" he asked, his voice faint.

Denny went pale. Maybe he hadn't meant to say it, or maybe he regretted it. But he kept talking.

"I think the other night in the water was the happiest I've ever been," he said. "And that's got to mean something."

Brian took a deep breath. "It doesn't have to mean love. We haven't known each other long enough for that. I mean, it's crazy."

Denny wasn't backing down. "Maybe not, if love is something rational. Is it?"

The breeze rustled through palm fronds above them, whispering some kind of secret Brian didn't understand. He was torn between the urge to wrap his arms around Denny in the tightest way possible and the instinct to flee, to get out of this parking lot, because he couldn't talk about love when he was still so angry about Denny's deception.

"I can't do this right now," he said. "I need some time."

He started to walk toward his car and was startled when Denny dashed forward and blocked him.

"I screwed up, and I'm sorry," he said. "Tell me what you want me to do."

Brian said, "It doesn't work like that. There's no magic fix-it when you hurt someone."

"But I want to try," Denny insisted. "Let me try."

"Don't go to your aunt's party," Brian said. "Skip it. Spend the day with me."

It was a terrible thing to ask, because Sean had said and Brian knew for sure how much family meant to Andersons. At the same time, Brian needed to know that he was important, too. That he mattered as much as family, especially if Denny was going to start throwing a word like *love* around. For a moment he thought Denny might even agree, and hope flared in his cold chest.

But Denny said, "I can't back out."

"But you can back out on me," Brian said, stung. "Thanks a lot. Get out of the way."

Denny didn't move.

"Go," Brian said, more sternly. Denny stepped aside. Brian got into his car and drove off and didn't look back; he didn't want to see Denny's expression, and at that moment didn't even care if he ever saw him again.

CHAPTER TWENTY-EIGHT

Steven decided that no trio of girls was ever going to scare him from his own turf. With Denny off in the bathroom, he got up from the booth and sauntered over to the round table. Well, sauntered as much as he could with a slightly gimpy knee. He ended up standing between Kelsey and Melissa, both of whom resolutely ignored his most charming smile.

"If it isn't Fisher Key's most amazingly beautiful ladies," he said.

"I hear a gnat," Jennifer said blithely.

"I hear a flea," Kelsey returned. "Maybe a flea on the back of a gnat."

Melissa consulted her phone. "I hear a tick on a flea on a gnat. Maybe we can get some pesticide with our salads."

Steven didn't let his smile dim a single watt. "Whatever microscopic insect I am, I can't stop thinking about any of you."

Kelsey picked up her glass of water. He eyed it warily, hoping she didn't throw it, but she only took a delicate sip.

"It's not a flea or a tick or a gnat," she said. "It's rat."

Melissa flicked Steven a disdainful gaze. "A large, smelly, diseased rat."

He thought that was harsh—he certainly didn't have any *diseases*.

"A rat that should sink with its ship," Jennifer added, and that didn't make much sense at all.

"Can't I sit down and explain?" he asked, using his best puppy-dog eyes. "Or are you just going to condemn a man without knowing the full story?"

The three of them exchanged silent looks.

"You can stand there and explain," Jennifer said archly. "You've got sixty seconds."

Steven dipped his head. "I guess it started when the tree fell on our house and I lost everything I owned. Then the SEALs told me I didn't pass the vision test, and they're not going to let me go to boot camp. Then Denny hired us out to this guy and his daughter, and they've been driving us nuts all week—"

Kelsey perked up. "Tristan! Jen, I told you about her. One minute she's completely nice and the next you think she's going to rip your head off."

Confused, Steven asked, "How do you know her?"

"I've been babysitting her little brother all week," Kelsey said. "I'm completely happy they're leaving tomorrow."

Melissa was giving Steven a sympathetic look. "I heard about your house. I didn't know you lost everything."

Jennifer asked, "Why didn't you tell us about the SEALs? They can't just not let you join now!"

Soon he was sitting at their table, sharing more of his woes, basking in some well-deserved sympathy. Several minutes passed before he realized that Sean and Brian had left and Denny had never come back from the bathroom. Louanne Garrity had brought his cheeseburger to his new seat, but Denny's food was untouched back in their booth.

Steven really hoped Denny wasn't hiding in a stall.

"Have you seen my brother?" he asked Louanne when she refilled their drinks.

"He left," she said. She hadn't completely warmed up to Steven, but was at least not frosty cold anymore. "I saw him crossing the highway a few minutes ago."

"Headed which way?"

"I am not your brother's keeper," she said.

Steven checked his phone—no messages—but didn't chase after him. He was still starving, and his cheeseburger tasted great (if a little charred), and Denny could take care of himself. Plus he couldn't be rude and leave the girls, right?

"What about the test tomorrow?" Jennifer asked. "Is anyone going with you?"

"The master chief recruiter will be there," Steven said.

Melissa volunteered, "I have to go up to Miami—I could drive you."

"No, I could drive him," Kelsey said.

"You have to babysit," Jennifer said sweetly. "I can do it."

Kelsey's gaze narrowed. "You promised not to push him."

"I'm not pushing," Jennifer said. "He can decide on his own."

"I can leave whenever you want, and I'm going up anyway," Melissa said helpfully.

Both Jennifer and Kelsey turned on her with venomous looks.

"I have to find Denny," Steven said, pushing back his chair. He dropped twenty dollars on the table. "I'll call you later."

"Call who?" they demanded.

He fled before he had to answer.

❖

Denny started walking. He didn't have any destination or goal in mind, just the urgent need to get away from all the bleeding pieces of his heart in the Li'l Conch parking lot.

You did this to yourself, he thought.

You shouldn't have lied.

He decided that relationships sucked. They tricked you with

promises of happiness and milestone events (eighteen days might as well be a thousand now, might as well be eternity) and ripped you up and spat you out. He'd been better off when he didn't have anything like a boyfriend. He should have stayed that way rather than risk the kind of pain he was experiencing now.

Denny walked and he walked, on roads he'd known all his life, past buildings and landmarks and trees burned into his brain, and felt relief that he'd be going away. Huge, incredible relief that he wouldn't have to stay and revisit the scenes of his own mistakes, over and over. Maybe he could even go to New London early. Take a bus up, find someplace cheap to stay... Brad's money would be put to good use, and make the whole week of diving worthwhile.

It was dark by the time he found himself standing outside the Bookmine. The lights were on in the upstairs apartment. He could see his mother up there, standing by the sink. He wanted to be mad at her for telling Brian but she hadn't known any better. Aunt Riza moved into his line of sight, bustling about with frying pan full of something. It was a lot easier to blame her. She'd forced him into a compromise he shouldn't have made. But he'd gone into it with his eyes open, and it wasn't her fault he'd screwed it up by lying to Brian.

Still, when Brian had essentially said *choose me or choose your family*, Denny hadn't been able to do it. Couldn't say he'd cancel the party. It was too important to both Aunt Riza and Mom.

With a sigh, he let himself into the closed store and punched the security code into the panel. The stacks were all dark except for some red emergency exit lighting. He got a flashlight from behind the counter and headed for the aisle about the military. Not history, not photography, but here, books about famous and not-so-famous Coast Guard rescues. He'd owned most of them but lost them when his and Steven's bedroom got drenched.

Denny sat down on the rugged floor, his back against the shelves, and started reading.

His phone beeped with a message from Steven: *where r u?*
Nowhere, Denny typed back. *Don't worry.*

Upstairs, a pair of footsteps moved across the floor. He ignored them. It was nice and dim and cool in the aisles, and he was happy to be alone.

r u sulking? Steven asked.

Denny ignored him.

He tried to concentrate on the story in front of him—two tankers sinking in a New England hurricane—but he kept thinking about Brian, and where Brian was right now, and if Brian really meant for him to go away forever, and what if Brian did end up dating Sean? That would be reason enough to never come back to Fisher Key.

A circle of light appeared at the end of the aisle, and then a flashlight beam found on him.

"What are you doing, Denny?" his mother asked.

Blinded, he raised a hand up. "Nothing."

Mom shifted her beam away and came to sit on the floor beside him. Her dark hair was loose around her shoulders and she was wearing the pink *Coast Guard Mom* T-shirt that Denny had bought her last Christmas.

"I was really quiet," he said. "How'd you know I was here?"

Mom said, "Your brother called. He thought maybe you had a fight with Brian and you'd come here."

"I don't want to talk about it."

"Good," she said. "Because, you know, moms are pretty awful when it comes to advice about emotions or love."

Denny went back to staring at the pages in his lap, although his vision had gone a little blurry. "You can't love someone you've only known for a few weeks."

Mom nodded sagely. "That's exactly what I told your father. Silly man."

Alarmed, Denny said, "You told him I had a fight with Brian?"

Her face scrunched up. "No, I'm talking about twenty-one years ago. When we met. We dated five times in two weeks and then he said he loved me. I said he was foolish."

Heavier footsteps thumped above them. Dad was home.

"Five dates isn't a lot," Denny said.

"I agree."

Denny was quiet for a moment. He could hear Mom breathing and smell her floral perfume, but she was quiet, too.

"What did Dad say?" he asked.

"He said that if you're a bowling pin in an alley, and a big twelve-pound ball smacks into you, you know it."

Skeptically, Denny asked, "Dad used a bowling analogy?"

"He was very big into bowling once," Mom said, as if sharing a special secret. "That was our first date. A bowling alley in Hialeah. I specialized in gutter balls and he broke two hundred."

"And still you got married," Denny said.

"After we dated for a year," she said.

"So love is like a bowling ball."

Mom patted his leg. "Love is what it is. Bowling ball, lightning strike, chemistry—it doesn't matter if you feel it right away or feel it after a year. You can't help it. And you don't want to. When you and Steven were born, I loved you the minute I stopped screaming in pain."

Denny winced. "Way to ruin the special moment, Mom."

"That's my job. Are you hungry? There's food upstairs with your name on it."

Denny thumped his head softly against the shelves. "I don't think I can deal with Aunt Riza right now."

"Hmm," she said. "If that's the case, I know a pizza place not too far away. You could walk me there, and I can pretend you're not going to be moving away in three weeks, right out of my life."

Mom said that last part cheerfully, but the expression on her face made his vision go watery again.

Denny reached forward and hugged her. He wanted to remember this: sitting in the bookstore that he'd practically grown up in, him and his small, strong, incredible mom.

"Let's get some pizza," he said. "My treat."

CHAPTER TWENTY-NINE

The only person on the island with a worse social life than Steven's was Eddie, so he went to Eddie's house and found him doing something completely out of character—cleaning the place from top to bottom.

"What is this?" Steven asked, standing in a kitchen filled with garbage bags. "Are you being evicted?"

Eddie was standing at the kitchen counter with his hands covered with dishwashing soap. "Very funny. Make yourself useful and haul those outside, why don't you?"

Steven liked being useful. He stashed the garbage bags in the outside bins and returned to see Eddie washing dishes as if his life depended on it.

"What's with the clean campaign?" Steven asked.

"My grandmother is coming from Columbus," Eddie said. "First time in twenty years. Mom says if we make a good impression, she'll give us money."

As far as motives went, it wasn't the best that Steven had ever heard. On the other hand, anything that got Eddie off the sofa and actually doing something was something to be applauded.

Eddie asked, "How do you feel about emptying the refrigerator?"

"I don't think our friendship could survive that," Steven said, frankly. He'd seen the shelves inside, and they reminded him of a toxic waste dump. "How about I do the dishes and you do the refrigerator?"

Ten minutes later, Steven's hands were lemon-smelling and starting to prune, while Eddie was tackling the refrigerator with a painter's mask over his face. Steven told him about the femme fatale trio of Jennifer, Kelsey, and Melissa, and Eddie said it was all very cruel.

"What's cruel? That I didn't call?"

"That you've got three otherwise smart girls fighting over you when they could be fighting over me," Eddie said.

The word "fighting" reminded Steven of Jamie Harrison. His knee was still sore, but some aspirin earlier was helping that. He told Eddie about the weather satellite and the *Othello II*, and how he expected Harrison to show up and cause trouble.

Eddie hauled out a plastic bowl of mold. "But he hasn't?"

"Not that I've seen."

"Do you think this bowl is worth saving?"

"I'll buy you another at the dollar store if you throw it away right now."

After a few hours' work the kitchen looked reasonably clean, although Steven decided that scrubbing the interior of the tomato-sauce-crusted microwave was outside of his job description. They ended up in the living room, moving aside piles of clothing and unopened mail so that they could watch TV.

"Have you considered the idea that maybe you and your mom are hoarders?" Steven asked.

"I think we're just slobs," Eddie said.

They watched TV and drank some beer and Steven could almost forget that tomorrow's vision test would determine his entire future and on Saturday he had to take a black belt test with Sensei Mike's "surprise" factored into the equation. He thought about telling Eddie about the test but didn't want to jinx himself. By midnight he was back on the *Idle*, where Denny was already sacked out and snoring.

Steven woke him up by shaking his shoulder.

"What?" Denny asked crankily, without opening his eyes.

"What if I don't pass tomorrow?" Steven asked.

"Huh?" Denny cracked open one eye. "You woke me up for that?"

It was dark on the boat and all over Fisher Key. Steven thought maybe the two of them were the only ones awake on the whole island. Which was silly, of course, but he couldn't shake the feeling.

"Yes, I woke you up for that," he said crossly.

Denny blinked at him. "If you don't pass you'll do something else. Haven't I already made five thousand suggestions?"

"You made three. Maybe four."

"Same thing. Go to sleep." Denny burrowed into his pillow, conversation over.

The next morning Steven swallowed more aspirin and ran two miles, which was hardly anything at all. His knee twinged once or twice, but seemed overall fine. He was showered and ready to leave by eight o'clock. The drive to Master Chief King's office wouldn't take that long, but who knew what might happen on the Overseas Highway—car accidents, jackknifed trucks, dead alligators, or maybe even a collapsed bridge or two.

Denny had slept in late and was drinking coffee as Steven triple-checked the directions on his phone.

"I could take it for you," Denny reminded him.

"I think Master Chief King would notice the difference."

"All I have to do is drop my IQ ten points," Denny said.

"You're pretty cheerful for someone whose heart got crushed," Steven said suspiciously.

Denny's smirk sobered up. "Thanks for reminding me."

"You didn't patch things up yet?"

"I don't think he wants to."

"Of course he wants to," Steven said. "Nobody dumps an Anderson. Take him out for a day at sea, do whatever you have to."

"I'll be sure to keep your advice in mind," Denny replied. His gaze went toward the parking lot. "Dad's here."

Steven squinted at the unmarked sedan the sheriff's office used. "Maybe he brought doughnuts."

"Maybe he wants to wish you good luck." Denny said.

When Steven went up to the parking lot, his father was waiting against the hood of the sedan. He was in uniform, no doughnuts, a calm look on his face.

"I thought maybe I'd drive you up there," he said. "Make sure you don't run into any trouble on the way."

Steven tried not to cringe. "Dad. I won't run into trouble."

"I didn't say I'd go to the appointment with you," Dad continued, as if he hadn't heard Steven at all. "Just drive you up there, do some work of my own, and drive you back."

Steven didn't know how to tell him it would be embarrassing. He opened his mouth, but Dad held up a forestalling hand.

"I know you don't need help," Dad said. "I know you can do it on your own. And I know you think maybe I'm treating you like a kid. But maybe I'm doing this for me, okay? I haven't seen you lately. I'd like to see you more before you go off to boot camp."

Steven bit back his surprise. "Dad, I might not pass. There might not be a boot camp at all."

Dad made a skeptical noise. "Steven, sooner or later, you're going to end up exactly where you belong. Maybe it's the SEALs, maybe it's the Marines, maybe it's the Coast Guard like your brother. But you're going to end up somewhere, and no stupid vision test is going to stand in your way."

Dad's confidence was kind of heartwarming. Steven felt himself blush.

"That doesn't mean you have to drive me," he muttered.

"Do your old man a favor and let him feel useful once in a while," Dad said.

Steven supposed that wasn't such a hardship after all.

"Okay," he said. "But if I pass, you're buying dinner."

"Deal," Dad said.

❖

Denny didn't quite know what to do with himself. He ruled out his first impulse, which was to crawl back into bed and ignore the world. He briefly considered his second, which was to go work at the Bookmine. But it was a gorgeous day for boating, with clear skies and a flawless forecast, and he didn't want to be cooped up all day. He needed the horizon and waves and so he'd take out the *Sleuth-hound*, maybe all the way up to Key Largo and back.

He called down to Sensei Mike's just to triple-check that everything was in order for their test tomorrow. An unfamiliar voice picked up.

"Yes?" the man asked. He sounded elderly, and his voice was heavily accented. Japanese, Denny thought. Denny asked for Sensei Mike and the man briefly considered his request.

"Yes," he said again, confidently.

"Is Mike there?" Denny asked.

"Yes," was the third reply.

"I'll call back," Denny said, and hung up.

Thirty seconds after disconnecting he put together Sensei's special surprise with the fact of an elderly Japanese visitor. He called Steven.

"What?" Steven asked.

"Sensei Enji," Denny said.

"You're not making any sense."

"I think the surprise tomorrow is Sensei Enji. Mike's sensei. Someone speaking Japanese just answered his phone."

Steven was silent for a minute. "I guess we better do really good tomorrow. Otherwise he'll kill us for embarrassing him."

Denny didn't think Sensei Mike would be embarrassed so much as disappointed, because it was one thing to flunk a couple of students on a test but quite another if your mentor was there to see the debacle. "When you come back we'll get in a few more hours of practice."

A few slips over, Larry Gold appeared on the deck of his boat, shirtless and yawning and scratching at his tanned belly. Tristan and Brad didn't seem to be on time this morning, either. Not Denny's problem. He had already told Steven he was borrowing the truck and so he loaded their scuba tanks in it, dropped them off at Darla Stewart's dive shop for refilling, and headed to the *Sleuth-hound*.

Brian didn't call him, didn't send a text message, didn't send a carrier pigeon or flare or smoke signals. Denny tried very hard not to think about it. Talking to Mom had helped more than he'd thought it would. Whatever he felt for Brian—felt strongly, felt like a knife under his ribs, felt like a big monster wave—he couldn't force Brian to feel it back, or to even accept it. He could just make amends somehow for being a lying jerk.

Two hours later, he was catching absolutely nothing at all and trying to figure out the whole amends thing when a distress call came over the radio.

"Help!" Tristan Flaherty said, her voice frantic. "Can anyone hear me? We need help!"

CHAPTER THIRTY

The Coast Guard answered Tristan's distress call, asking her
what the emergency was.

"My dad hit his head and he's bleeding," she said. "Our captain
pulled him out of the water but he's got chest pains and his lips are
turning blue."

"Where are you located?" the Coast Guard operator asked.

The *Agana*, Denny thought immediately.

"I'm not sure," Tristan said. "We were diving this old military
ship, the *Agana*—"

Denny was already throttling up the *Sleuth-Hound*.

He was only a mile or so from the spot, and so was first on
the scene. Tristan waved frantically from the deck as he tied up
alongside. Larry Gold was flat on his back as she gave him CPR.
Brad was on the dive platform but unable to haul himself over the
railing. He had a nasty gash on his forehead and a glazed sheen to
his eyes.

Denny said, "Can you keep holding on?" and Brad nodded,
but Denny had his doubts. His hands were trembling and the waves
were lifting and dropping him, tugging him away.

"Help Dad," Tristan said. She was doing compressions, fast and
hard, the same way Denny had learned, and counting loud. "Twenty,
twenty-one, twenty-two—I've got this."

Denny got Brad onto the boat and settled in a corner. Despite the warm temperature, he was shivering, and one of his pupils was wider than the other. Concussion and shock, Denny thought. A first aid kit was open on the deck, the contents scattered everywhere. He ripped open a large bandage, got it up close and personal against the gash, and said, "Hold this tight. Stay on your side, in case you throw up."

"Bossy kid," Brad said, but did as told.

Denny took over the compressions and Tristan did the rescue breathing, using the disposable mask from the first aid kit to force air into Larry's lungs. His face was gray and clammy. Denny's compressions and Tristan's air were the only thing keeping him alive.

The steady thump of rotors registered on Denny's ears, quickly growing louder as the Coast Guard Jayhawk helicopter arrived. The whirling air made loose supplies go skittering across the deck. A rescue swimmer dropped into the waves and a few strokes later was hauling himself up into the boat.

Denny recognized him instantly: AST Third Class Eric Beamer, who'd run the Seven Mile Bridge marathon last year and almost beaten Steven. Almost.

"How's it looking?" Eric asked, feeling for Larry's pulse.

"Not so good," Denny said honestly. The compressions strained his arms, but he kept at them. "We've got two patients for you."

"I'm fine," Brad insisted over the noise of the chopper.

Tristan said, "You're not, Dad!"

"He's paraplegic and he's got a concussion," Denny told Eric.

Eric did a quick assessment on Brad, despite Brad's protests. The expression on his face was not encouraging. His crewmates aboard the chopper sent down a gurney for Larry. They used a strop to lift Brad. Tristan wanted to go with them but it was more important to get the patients to Fisherman's Hospital than to waste time hauling her up, too.

Eric waved from the open door once Brad was aboard. The chopper zoomed off, quickly becoming an orange-white dot on the horizon.

"I'll take you up there," Denny promised. "Your dad will be fine."

He steered Larry's boat back toward home with the *Sleuthhound* towed behind her. Tristan was unnaturally quiet, definitely shaken up, but she went down below and put on dry clothing. She stuffed her father's wallet, phone, and medicine into a backpack, grabbed another bag with her own belongings inside, and cleaned up the deck of Larry's boat. She called the hospital as soon as they were in range of a cell phone tower. The admitting clerk in the ER had nothing to tell her.

"What if he needs me?" Tristan fretted. "He doesn't always tell doctors the truth, and he's stubborn—"

"We'll be there in twenty minutes," Denny promised.

Back home, he slid behind the wheel of Steven's truck and waited until they were on the road before asking, "What happened out there?"

"We did the dive," she said. "The currents were pretty strong, like you said. I had to hold on to the guidelines with both hands, most of the time—but it was okay, we didn't do anything wrong. We didn't stay down too long. When we came back up, Dad slipped while pulling himself up. He banged his head and fell back into the water. Larry went in and pulled him out, but something was wrong—he was clutching his arm and he couldn't breathe."

"Gave himself a heart attack," Denny said.

Tristan said, "It could have happened to anyone. It was just a stupid accident."

Denny didn't argue with her. He may have broken a speed limit or two on the way to Islamorada, but Tristan wasn't complaining. Once they reached the emergency room, she tried to argue her way past the clerk to be with her dad.

"The doctor will be right out," the admitting nurse promised.

In Denny's experience, that was never true. But Tristan couldn't win the argument, so they sat in the blue plastic chairs and waited. Tristan stared at the white-and-green wall as if imagining the very worst possible scenario.

"Shouldn't you call your mom?" he asked.

"He'd hate that," Tristan said. "He'd absolutely kill me for worrying her."

Up on the wall, a flat-screen TV was showing some inane reality show about Hollywood socialites. Denny checked his watch. Steven should be taking his test by now.

"You don't have to stay," Tristan said.

"No, I'll stay," he said. "I'm just thinking about Steven's test."

"The vision thing?"

"The really important vision thing. Otherwise they won't let him in."

"He really wants it," she said.

"Yeah. He really does. As much as I want to go into the Coast Guard."

She was staring at the wall again. "I wish I felt that strongly about something."

"I thought you loved astronomy," he said.

"I used to think I did," she replied. "All summer long I'd lie on our roof and watch the stars while my parents argued about stuff. I made up my own constellations: Peaceful Dog, Zen Cat, Gate to Forgiveness. I even made up a spreadsheet."

Denny leaned forward, his elbows on his knees. "So what happened?"

"We started scuba diving. And I thought, maybe the answer's not out there at all. Maybe it's down in the water."

He chose his next words carefully. "Or maybe you want diving to be important to you because it's important to your father."

She didn't argue.

After another half hour of waiting, a doctor finally came out to tell them Brad was mostly fine. "We'll keep him tonight, keep an eye on that hard head, but he's a tough guy."

"What about Larry Gold?" Denny asked. "He had the heart attack. We gave him CPR."

"Still hanging in, I think," the doctor said, but didn't sound hopeful.

When they were allowed to see Brad, he was sitting up in bed looking disgruntled. Tristan flung herself at him and he rubbed her back soothingly.

"I know," he said. "Stupid accident."

"You're not forgiven," Tristan muttered.

Brad met Denny's gaze. "Thanks for all your help out there."

"No problem."

"Doesn't mean you were right about diving the *Agana*," Brad reminded him. "I got some great shots."

"Let's not talk about it," Tristan said, wiping her eyes. "I'm too traumatized."

Denny stayed for only a few minutes. He offered to take Tristan back to Fisher Key but she wanted to spend the night on the pull-out futon and wouldn't be dissuaded, as stubborn as her father. Denny was two miles away from the hospital when he heard a rattling and pulled over to investigate. Tristan's inexpensive digital camera had fallen out of her bag on the drive up. He called her and offered to bring it back.

"I'll pick it up from you later," she said. "Check out my awesome shots."

She sounded like her mood was back on the upswing. Denny hung up and turned on the camera. He recognized the *Agana*'s bow, and there was her upper deck, encrusted with sea life and coral, the railings rusting to nothingness. Tristan had captured shots of the ocean floor, nothing particularly unique about them, except for one rectangular metal object he couldn't quite identify.

Denny stared at for a moment, puzzling. It looked battered, but not like it had been submerged long.

His phone rang. It was Darla Stewart's shop, telling him his tanks were ready. He put Tristan's camera aside and promptly forgot all about it.

❖

They arrived in Miami with a lot of time to kill. Dad bought them an early lunch at McDonald's but Steven could only pick at his cheeseburger. Dad read the paper and Steven surfed the net on his phone. When it came time to drop Steven off, Dad stuck to his word and didn't try to come in. Instead, he said he'd be back in a couple of hours, and added "Good luck" about twelve times.

"See you later, Dad," Steven said.

He had butterflies in his stomach when he pushed open the doors to the recruiting office. *Nothing to worry about*, he told himself. *Just my entire future. Red, blue, green, yellow—how hard can it be?*

A cold wave of air-conditioning hit him, and goose bumps rose on his arms.

"Steven Anderson for Master Chief King," he told the yeoman at the front desk.

"I see you, recruit!" King bellowed from his corner desk. "Come on back here, Mr. Can't See Blue and Green."

That was the nice thing about Master Chief King—he didn't beat around the bush. He was black, six foot two, and completely bald, with the same stocky build Steven's father had. Steven had never asked him if he'd played football, but he certainly wouldn't want to be on the field opposite him.

"Nervous?" he asked as Steven shook his hand.

"Not much," Steven replied.

Master Chief nodded. "What do you do with a blue whale?"

Steven was flummoxed. "What?"

"You cheer him up!" Master Chief King said. "What's orange and sounds like a parrot?"

"I don't know," Steven admitted.

"A carrot!"

With a perfectly straight face, Steven said, "Very funny, Master Chief."

King grinned. "It's an eight-mile drive to the doctor at MEPS and believe you me, I've got dozens of them."

"We know he does," said the recruiter at the next desk dryly. "He's been practicing them all week."

The jokes weren't very good, but they were a nice distraction. At MEPS Steven was ushered past the doctors he'd seen for his first physical and taken down to the ophthalmologist, a civilian named Dr. Meadows.

"Doc, let me tell you about this kid," Master Chief King said. "He did the PST swim in 7:48. He did the run in 9:40. He can sit-up and push-up and stand up better than any recruit I've seen in the last five years. He's not color-blind."

Dr. Meadows, who was slight and pale and scrawny, took Steven's folder from his assistant and said, "I hope not. Come on this way, Mr. Anderson."

Steven followed him into an examination room. Dr. Meadows had him sit in the big chair and took a rolling stool for himself. The office was mostly bare, except for an eye chart on the wall and a stack of recruiting folders on the counter.

"So you failed the FALANT," Dr. Meadows said, studying Steven's file. He didn't sound particularly concerned or interested. In fact, he sounded like he was thinking of dinner with his wife or a good movie he wanted to see.

"Yes, sir," Steven said. "But I tried it at my regular eye doctor's office last month, and he said it was fine."

"The civilian version's a little different," Dr. Meadows said. He kept reading.

Steven studied the chart, then the back of the door, then the ceiling tiles.

"Do you know how it's scored?" Dr. Meadows asked, flipping a page.

"Yes, sir. If I pass all nine light combinations in the first run, I'm good. If I miss one, I get two more tries at it."

Dr. Meadows said, "You missed three the last time. But you say you did fine at your regular doctor's."

"That's right."

"Were you rushing when you took it here?"

Steven said, "I don't think so."

"Were you nervous?"

"Not then." In fact, Steven distinctly remembered being completely relaxed and confident. Maybe too confident. "But to tell the truth, I'm nervous now."

Dr. Meadows lifted his head and gave Steven a sympathetic smile. "It's a big thing. Huge, right? I'm going to tell you right now, this machine is the best model from here to Norfolk. It's been calibrated and recalibrated and fine-tuned to the umpteenth degree. We believe in the machine, Steven. We trust it."

"Yes, sir," Steven said, but meanwhile he was thinking: *Never trust a machine.*

"Good," Dr. Meadows said. "Let's start."

CHAPTER THIRTY-ONE

Brian didn't sleep at all Thursday night. He didn't have much appetite for breakfast, and he couldn't think of a single thing to do with himself other than throw himself back into the final pages of *Duma Key*. The words kept slipping off the page and he consistently lost track of what was going on.

You can't love someone when you've only known them for four weeks, he told himself. *That's too soon.*

You're a jerk, Denny Anderson.

Sean called him around noon. "Are you going to keep me in suspense all day?"

He went out on the balcony and gazed at the flat, shimmering Gulf of Mexico. "About that?"

"About what?" Sean's voice squeaked. "How about the parking lot of reconciliation? His big fat apology and how you took it?"

"He didn't exactly apologize," Brian said.

"He didn't?"

"And he didn't invite me to his aunt's party."

"That's what you want? To meet his hundred Cuban cousins and aunts and uncles?"

"Sure."

"Let me ask you something. Do you want to be there for him, or to be there for yourself?"

Brian bristled. "It's not about me."

"Yeah, that's right. It's not about you," Sean said, exasperated. "He's only going for his mom and aunt. You may not have noticed, but Steven's the glory hound and Denny's happy to take no credit at all."

"He doesn't have to go."

"So you want him to hurt his mom to make you feel better?"

Brian didn't like Sean's tone or oversimplification. He stared at the horizon, and listened to the laughter of people in the pool down below, and smelled barbecue on the breeze.

"He lied to me," he said. *And he said the L-word.*

"Which sucks, but doesn't mean you have to end everything. If I had a boyfriend like Denny Anderson, I'd give him a second chance. Or maybe a third, or a fourth, or whatever, but don't hold a grudge."

After they hung up Brian thought about that word, *grudge*, and dialed Denny's number.

Denny answered, "Hello?" and it was a cautious word, as if he expected something worse.

Brian leaned on the railing. "Hey. When are you going down to Key West tonight?"

"I don't know. Depends on when Steven gets back from Miami."

"Do you want to eat dinner early somewhere?"

A pause. Brian could hear music and traffic in the background.

"Yeah, definitely," Denny said. "I'm on my way back from Islamorada. I've got to take care of the boats. I can pick you up around five?"

"Okay," Brian said. "Five."

Neither of them hung up right away. Brian wasn't sure what to say, even as words flitted through his mind: *you're a jerk* and *you drive me crazy* and *don't lie to me*, and maybe *what does love mean to you?*

"I'll see you later," Brian said. "I'm glad we're going out."

"I'm glad, too," Denny replied, and Brian was sure he was smiling.

❖

As Denny pulled into the parking lot of Darla Stewart's dive shop he knew he had a silly grin on his face, but he couldn't help it. Not only had Brian called him, but he'd wanted to go to dinner, and he'd said he was *glad* they were going out. So that was a good thing, right? If Brian never wanted to see him again, all he had to do was say so over the phone.

The shop was empty when Denny let himself in. Darla was behind the counter, testing a regulator, her face furrowed in a frown.

"You look unhappy, Chief," Denny said. Everyone called her Chief, even though she was long retired.

"This thing is a piece of junk." She dropped the regulator into a cardboard box. Her keen eyes assessed him. "I heard you had some excitement this morning, huh?"

"That's pretty fast news," Denny said.

"Larry Gold's damn lucky you were around."

"It wasn't me who saved him. Tristan Flaherty started CPR before I got there."

"Always modest," Darla replied. "Your tanks are all set."

"Thanks," he said.

The dive shop was adjacent to Mac's Marine Repairs. As he loaded the tanks into Steven's truck he saw the *Othello II* docked at one of the piers and remembered what Claire had said about the crew going back to Virginia. When he climbed into the driver's seat his leg brushed against Tristan's camera, with its photo of the mystery object near the wreck of the *Agana*.

He drove into the yard and found Red Sox Bud on the deck, hosing off some gear.

"Denny or Steven?" Bud asked.

"Denny," he said. "I thought everyone went home."

"Someone's got to stay with the baby," Bud said, sounding disgruntled. "What's up?"

"I have some pictures I thought you could look at," Denny said. "Maybe it's nothing, but something weird showed up."

"Sure. Come aboard."

They went down below decks to the tiny galley. The boat was empty. Bud offered him coffee, but Denny thought he'd save it for dinner with Brian. Bud thumbed through the photos on Tristan's camera, his eyebrows pulled together in concentration.

"These were shot today?" he asked.

"This morning."

"Exactly where?"

"A few miles offshore," Denny said. "Do you think that's part of that satellite that came down?"

Bud grunted. "Hard to say. Did you show these to anyone else?"

"Not yet."

"I'll download them and take a closer look, if that's okay."

"Sure."

Bud got his laptop and inserted the memory card from Tristan's camera. As he peered more closely at the images, Denny's phone buzzed with a text message from Steven:

!!!!!!!!!!

Denny squinted at the screen and typed back *?????that better be yes u passed.*

"I think you found something interesting," Bud said. "Can you take me out there?"

"Yeah, sure," Denny said. He didn't bother correcting him that Tristan found it. "But tomorrow I'll be in Key West, so it'll have to be early Sunday morning."

"If you give me the GPS coordinates, I can get another diver," Bud said intently. He popped out the memory card and put it back in

Tristan's camera. "Better not to let it sit in the salt water too long, if it is what I think it is."

Denny picked up the camera. "Sure. I'll send them when I get back home."

"Ballpark figures?" Bud asked. "I hate to wait."

A frisson ran up Denny's spine. Bud was being just a little too intent about it, a little too forward.

"I don't know them offhand," Denny said. "I've got to go—my brother's waiting for me."

Bud closed the laptop. "Okay. Give me a call. NASA will be pretty happy if you've found what we're missing."

The intent stare was gone. Denny told himself he'd been overreacting. He was plugging Bud's number into his phone just as Steven sent: *totally aced it.*

"I'll call you," Denny said. "I know the way out."

He left the galley and headed for the ladder, thumbing in: *knew it.*

Three steps later, something hard slammed into the back of his head and sent the world rushing into darkness.

CHAPTER THIRTY-TWO

D ad was waiting in the parking lot.
   "So?" he asked.
Steven shuffled toward him with a perfectly hangdog face.
Dad's face fell. "I'm sorry, kiddo."
"I passed," Steven replied, grinning wildly.

With a whoop, Dad grabbed him and lifted him off his feet. Which was no easy task, but Dad managed anyway. And Steven didn't mind at all, because he felt happy enough to just float off into the sky anyway, one big balloon of happiness and relief.

"Perfect score," Steven said, as Dad squeezed the air out of him. "Perfect!"

"I knew it!" Dad put him down but kept his arms around him. "Color-blind, my ass."

Steven allowed himself one minute of holding tight, and manfully broke away.

"Well, you know," he said, and wished the sun wasn't so damned bright. "I never had any doubt."

On the way out of the parking lot he texted Denny a bunch of exclamation marks. Denny sent back a terse message. Steven grinned and sent *totally aced it*. Meanwhile he told Dad all about the test and Dr. Meadows and how Master Chief King had let out such a yell of "Yes!" that the whole building had heard him.

"Call your mom," Dad said. "She's going to cry."

Mom did cry, which was okay. Moms were allowed to cry when they were happy for you. Denny sent back *knew it*, which was kind of pithy, but Steven could forgive him because this was the best day of his life: He'd passed, he was going to be a SEAL, absolutely nothing could stop him now.

Before heading back to Fisher Key they had to stop off at the martial arts store in Homestead. Dad paid for the uniforms, saying it was his treat. Steven hoped to run them through a washing machine and dryer at least once, and when they got to Key West tonight they'd get a set of the dojo's patches to sew on.

"Do they let spectators watch the black belt test?" Dad asked.

"From the office, yeah," Steven said. "You want to come?"

"Your mother and aunt and I."

"It's pretty long and boring."

"Not to us. What time are you two leaving tonight, and where are you staying?"

"We were going to spring for a real hotel room, but I don't know when. I'll find out."

Denny didn't pick up. Steven hoped that meant he was off with Brian somewhere, fixing that mess, so he wouldn't be distracted during the test. From Homestead to Fisher Key it would be two hours, a straight shot. Steven begged to drive, but Dad said he'd rather avoid being pulled over, thank you very much.

"When did they say you start?" Dad asked.

"Training starts August third," Steven said. "I wish it started Monday."

"Boot camp in August. That'll be fun."

"Cakewalk, Dad."

The highway was clear until they reached Key Largo, when it slowed to a crawl. Dad got on the radio and found out there was a three-car accident north of Tavernier blocking the highway. It took them an hour to cover the next three miles. Steven tapped his foot, drummed on the dashboard, and compulsively checked his watch.

"Relax," Dad said. "It's out of your control."

"Fifty miles, and it's going to take us forever." Steven tried dialing Denny again, but still no answer. He called Brian.

"He's picking me up at five," Brian said. "We're going to dinner."

Steven had not authorized Denny to take his truck on a dinner date. Still, he could afford to be magnanimous. "Tell him I'm going to Eddie's to wash the uniforms, and he better pick me up when you guys are done."

"Got it," Brian said.

"And tell him to answer his phone once in a while."

The accident kept them crawling until the lanes opened up at four o'clock. Dad dropped Steven off at Eddie's. The house was even cleaner than when Steven had last visited, but Eddie didn't look happy. He was sitting at the kitchen table with a glum expression, filling out a job application.

"I need your washing machine," Steven said, and dumped the uniforms in the machine next to the sink. He threw in a cup of detergent, too. "What's the application for?"

"My uncle's car dealership."

"You don't have an uncle with a car dealership in the Florida Keys."

"It's in Columbus," Eddie said. "My grandmother wants me to move up there with her for a while."

"Since when do you want to sell cars in Columbus?"

"Since absolutely never," Eddie said. "How did your test go?"

Steven beamed at him.

"You dog," Eddie said.

They ordered a celebratory pizza to mark the occasion. Eddie offered up some beer, but Steven decided he'd better keep his head clear. Eddie drank two with dinner and then another while they watched a movie. Steven kept checking the time, wondering just how long Denny and Brian could make dinner last. His brother better not be off making out somewhere.

By eight o'clock he was calling Denny every fifteen minutes just to be annoying.

"My mom and grandma should be back soon," Eddie said. "You want to stick around and meet the Terror of Ohio?"

"I think I'll pass," Steven said.

"You want a ride back?"

"No. I'll walk."

He was furious with Denny, but the exercise might help him clear his head. It wasn't far—nothing on Fisher Key was far—but it was getting dark, he was tired, and his knee was stiff. This side of the island didn't have streetlights, but all he had to do was follow South Road around the point toward the marina, crossing Jeffers Bridge along the way.

Every few minutes he dialed Denny and left another snarky message.

"I hope you're having a really good time with your boyfriend and my truck," he said.

And then, "You know, the truck I pay for with my own money every month."

And also, "Remember my truck? You're never borrowing it again for the rest of your life, got it?"

No houses along here, just mangroves and marsh and the occasional whoosh of a car on the nearby Overseas Highway. Stars glittered overhead and waves washed up against the thin strip of shoreline. Steven didn't know if he could ever live in a city, with traffic and pollution and people jammed together in high-rises. He wasn't even sure what to expect on a big military base, only what he'd read or watched in movies—barracks, chow halls, reveille every morning, everything rigid and orderly. No palm trees or salty breezes, no chirp of a million insects on the road.

Jeffers Bridge was a concrete stretch that crossed over one of the largest inlets on the island. As Steven started across, headlights came up behind him and turned his silhouette into a long shadow. He turned and shielded his eyes against the glare. At first he thought it was Denny catching up with him, but the engine noise wasn't quite right. Maybe it was another local and he could hitch a ride—

The engine revved.

The headlights switched to high beams. The driver gunned straight toward him.

Steven dropped the karate uniforms and started to run.

But even as he sprinted, he knew he wasn't going to make it. The bridge was too long and the SUV too fast. In just a few seconds, Steven was going to be a large splat of road kill. Wouldn't that suck rotten eggs? His entire life, over before he even got to the good parts.

He veered toward the bridge railing, got his hands on the rusty metal, and swung himself over the side. For a few brief seconds there was only the panic of being in midair and falling helplessly, a total victim of gravity. Then he hit the warm water, sank over his head, and kicked to the surface. The outgoing current dragged him under the bridge. He grabbed for a pylon and clung tight, though sea moss made it slippery.

Above him, brakes screeched. Steven listened hard but the concrete muffled other noises. A few seconds later, the beam from a flashlight sliced down into the water just a few feet away and a man's voice yelled, "Nice try, kid! Get back up here!"

Steven kept silent. But he knew that voice. Placed it immediately.

The white beam swung closer.

Jamie Harrison said, "Show yourself and say hi to your brother, or I'll put this bullet right through his head."

CHAPTER THIRTY-THREE

Denny had woken up somewhere dark, cramped and reeking of bleach. His head ached and his wrists were zip-tied behind his back. He tried to move his feet and found them bound together as well.

So not good, he thought to himself.

He could reach his back pockets, and with some twisting around could pat down his front pockets as well. No cell phone, no pocketknife, not even the keys to Steven's truck. He struggled to sit up, but the movement made his stomach lurch and his head pound, and he ended up vomiting a thin stream of bile into his own lap.

For a moment the best he could do was rest his head against the cool bulkhead beside him. His heartbeat drowned out all other noises until they gradually asserted themselves: running water, a faraway murmured voice, a clang of metal.

Denny figured he was still on the *Othello II*. Bud would be nearby, along with whoever had hit him from behind.

He kicked out and yelled, "Hey! Let me out!"

No one came for him. Now that his eyes were growing accustomed to the dark, he could see that the door was not watertight. A thin rectangle of light seeped through the cracks. He kicked again, hoping maybe to break the lock. Shocks ran up his leg and into his back, but he braced himself and tried again.

After several minutes of futility, footsteps approached and the door swung open. Denny squinted against the blinding light, which made his head hurt a dozen times more.

"Shut up unless you want a bullet in the head," said Jamie Harrison, and the gun in his hand backed up the threat.

Denny responded by throwing up again. He wasn't sure, but he thought he got some on Harrison's pants.

Harrison swore at him and stalked away. A moment or two later, he came back with Bud in tow.

Bud crouched down and said, "You can make all the noise you want, kid. No one's going to hear you."

Denny had nothing left to vomit, but his stomach didn't know that. Dry heaves were no more fun than bile.

Bud said to Harrison, "You shouldn't have hit him so hard. How's he going to show us the site if he can't dive?"

"All we need are the coordinates," Harrison said.

"Where?" Denny croaked out.

Bud turned back to him. "Where those pictures were taken. Tell us where, and we'll leave you here. We'll call the cops in the morning and let them know where you are."

Denny stared at them in confusion. "Coordinates where?"

"The dive site," Bud said.

His stomach lurched again, and he curled into himself with a suitably pitiful groan.

Neither Bud nor Harrison seemed pleased. They didn't move him from the utility closet, but Bud got him some water and a handful of aspirin. Denny would rather have a knife to cut himself free, but he didn't think they'd comply if he asked. He didn't know how long he'd been unconscious but surely Steven was worried by now about his truck, if nothing else.

"He's fine," Harrison said nearby. "He's faking it."

"You probably broke his skull," Bud said. "Great going. A cop's kid, too."

"It's not going to matter once we've got the more," Harrison said.

That didn't make sense—*the more?*—but Denny couldn't ask about it. He kept his face pressed to the cool metal and tried to breathe steadily through his nose. He wished they would turn out the lights, at least.

"Let me see the pictures again," Harrison said.

They walked off down the corridor. Denny tried twisting his hands free, but zip ties were appallingly effective. He didn't think they'd be able to identify the *Agana* from Tristan's pictures. She hadn't taken any wide shots of the ship itself, only hatches and fish and the sandy bottom.

But when they came back, they had a plan.

"You might not be able to dive, but your boat GPS can show us the way," Harrison said. "You're coming along as insurance."

They cut his ankles loose and hauled him upward. He let his knees buckle and he sagged against Bud. Bud cursed again at Harrison for excessive force.

"I can't help it if his head is made of eggshells," Harrison retorted.

Bud cut his wrists loose. Denny would have taken the opportunity to fight, but the odds were too heavily against him. Even Steven would have thought twice in his situation.

"We're going to walk to the van, and you're not going to cause any trouble," he said. "Anyone who shows up is going to get shot, and it'll be on your shoulders."

It was night outside, with a stiff breeze from the west. The darkness worried Denny. He'd been unconscious longer than he thought. He hoped Brian wasn't too pissed he'd missed their dinner date. By now, though, maybe Steven would have persuaded Dad to activate the theft tracker in his truck, and they'd traced it here.

He didn't see the truck, though. Steven would be totally furious if Harrison had dumped it somewhere, such as off a bridge.

The marine yard had closed down for the day, leaving no one around to see Bud open the back doors of a dark-colored van. Denny was forced inside amid an impressive array of dive equipment. He sagged down on a dirty rug that smelled like engine oil and tried not to gag again. They left his feet unbound. Bud climbed in beside him and Harrison took the wheel.

"Ten million dollars, here we come," Harrison said.

CHAPTER THIRTY-FOUR

Brian was angry at Denny for blowing off their dinner date.

"Maybe he got stuck somewhere," Sean said at five thirty, when Brian called to complain.

By six o'clock it was pretty obvious Denny wasn't coming. Brian kicked himself for even suggesting it. He locked himself in his room, buried himself in a book, and vowed never to speak to Denny again in his entire life. When his phone started ringing with calls from Steven, Brian extended the ban to any Anderson on the planet.

Mom ordered them room service and tried to coax him into eating, but he refused.

"I'm not hungry," he said.

"You can't sulk in your room forever," she told him.

Brian sighed. "Sure I can."

But sulking was a kid's game—a stupid response that wore out quickly. Around eight p.m., he borrowed his mother's car and drove over to the marina. He'd make Denny explain himself in person. However, the *Idle* was dark and empty. He waited there for a while, but twilight came, and then darkness, and still no Denny. The anger in Brian's gut turned to worry. He went to the Bookmine and knocked on the apartment door.

"Come in!" Mrs. Anderson called out.

Brian took the stairs two at a time. The apartment looked homier than he'd last seen it, but he wasn't interested much in decor. Mrs. Anderson and her sister were watching a tiny TV set on the kitchen table.

"I'm looking for Denny," he said.

"He's not here," Mrs. Anderson said. "Did you try his cell phone?"

"He's not answering," Brian replied. "He was supposed to pick me up at five, but he didn't show up."

Mrs. Anderson picked up her phone and dialed Denny. No answer.

"He might have broken his phone again," she said.

"That doesn't explain why he missed our date," Brian said. "I'm starting to get really worried."

Aunt Riza gave him an appraising look. "Maybe he changed his mind."

"He would have told me," Brian insisted.

"I'll call my husband," Mrs. Anderson said.

"I'll keep looking," Brian said, resolute, and on the way back to his mother's car he called Sean again.

Sean said, "I knew Denny wouldn't just blow you off! He's got to be in trouble somewhere."

"Trouble how?" Brian asked.

"I don't know. But come pick me up and we'll drive around every place he could be."

"You really think he's in trouble?"

"It's been five whole days since a tree fell on them," Sean said. "It's time for another disaster."

❖

Steven wasn't sure Harrison's threat was real until he heard a distant yelp of pain that certainly sounded like Denny. Standing in the water under Jeffers Bridge, he clenched his fists and tried to figure out some heroic, impossible rescue.

"Come on, Steven!" That was Bud the Red Sox guy. "You can't win by staying down there."

Reluctantly Steven agreed. He called up with, "All right, I'm coming," and made his way up the slippery bank.

Bud and Harrison were waiting for him. Harrison was carrying a pistol and Bud had a flashlight. Steven stopped near the railing, hands up, waiting to see if he'd get shot.

"Don't be stupid," Bud said, "and you'll both live through the night."

Steven said, "You're sure about that?"

Harrison waved the gun toward the open back doors of the van. "Come on, hero boy. Get in."

Denny was inside, lying on his side, looking like crap in the dim light from the dome fixture. He was tied up and smelled like puke and squinted at Steven in an unhappy way.

"You should have run," he rasped out.

"Now you tell me," Steven said.

Harrison poked Steven in the back. "Shut up and climb in."

Steven gingerly stepped over Denny and the diving equipment. Bud climbed in right after him. Harrison slammed the doors, got behind the steering wheel, and started driving.

"Where are we going?" Steven asked.

"Not your problem," Bud said.

Totally my problem, Steven thought.

"They're looking for something," Denny said, sounding confused. "I don't know what."

Bud said, "Jamie was too zealous with a wrench."

The van stopped a mile later. Steven could see his own house through the back window. He had no idea why Larry Gold's boat was tied alongside the *Sleuth-hound*, and was further confused when Harrison and Bud ordered him to carry their dive equipment to it.

"Going somewhere?" Steven asked.

"We all are," Harrison smirked.

Under gunpoint Steven was told to help Denny to Larry's boat as well. Denny was unsteady on his feet, and stopped once with his hands on his knees as if he was going to throw up.

"He needs a hospital," Steven said.

"Later," Harrison snapped.

Steven didn't think there was going to be a later, not with Harrison and that gun around. But he couldn't take on two men at once, and he couldn't count on Denny to help. He wasn't about to run off and leave Denny alone with them, either.

"I'm fine," Denny rasped out. "What day is it?"

Once they were aboard Larry's boat, Bud told Steven to sit Denny on the deck and to keep quiet. Steven did as told. He kept Denny upright and felt along the back of his head. Bud hadn't been kidding about the wrench. There was a big goose-egg bump on the back of Denny's head, which explained a lot.

"Can you swim?" Steve murmured to him.

"Sure," Denny said.

Harrison was busy on the *Sleuth-hound*, fiddling with Denny's GPS. Bud kept glancing nervously toward shore, as if expecting the police to show up at any minute. Which Steven thought would be a great development, but he wasn't very hopeful about it.

Harrison came back to Larry's boat and checked his GPS as well. "They've both got the same spot in their history," he said. "A few miles out, like the kid said."

"What's a few miles out?" Steven asked.

"The more," Denny muttered, which didn't make sense.

"You'll see when we get there," Bud said. "You and Jamie are going to go for a nice midnight dive."

❖

Brian picked Sean up at Sean's house, which was a modest concrete block ranch set in a neighborhood of similar houses.

"What's the last thing Denny said to you?" Sean asked.

"I don't know. That he'd see me at five."

"Anything else?"

Brian stared through the windshield without seeing anything. "Something about the taking care of the boat. No, *boats*. More than one."

"Denny helped rescue Larry Gold this morning. Maybe he meant Larry's boat."

"Rescue?" Brian asked. "What rescue?"

"Heart attack while Larry had Brad and Tristan Flaherty out on a dive. I don't know much more about it."

Trust Denny to be a hero and not mention anything about it. Brian started driving back toward the marina.

"She's probably up in the hospital in Islamorada," Sean said. "I'll call her."

Once they were connected, Sean put her on his speakerphone. Tristan said, "I just talked to Sheriff Anderson. I haven't heard from Denny since he left around two thirty."

"Nothing at all?" Brian asked.

"He called and said I left my camera in his truck. That's it."

"Was there anything special on your camera?" Brian pressed. "Any strange pictures?"

Tristan made a huffing noise. "No, just fish and water and the wreck."

Sean asked, "What about the rest of your equipment? Where's that?"

"On Larry's boat," Tristan said. "We left it at Denny's house."

The Anderson house was dark and unoccupied. Brian wasn't sure the power had been restored yet. An empty van was parked on the grass. The *Sleuth-hound* was exactly where she should be, but Larry's boat was gone.

"We better call Sheriff Anderson," Sean said.

Brian squinted at the dark sea and sky and shivered with foreboding. *Denny, where are you?*

CHAPTER THIRTY-FIVE

The wind off the water was cold enough to raise goose
bumps on Denny's arms. It didn't help that he was tucked
beside Steven, who was wet from swimming under Jeffers Bridge
and had to be even colder than Denny.

Steven didn't shiver, though. He was watching Bud and
Harrison sharply, waiting for some kind of opening.

Denny wanted to say *Don't be an idiot*, but he didn't want Bud
glancing their way. As far as Bud knew, Denny still had his brains
scrambled from Harrison's wrench. But the aspirin had helped,
Denny had been faking the amnesia part anyway, and at least half
the vomiting had been a ruse.

But the other half of it hadn't been faked at all. The rock and
sway as Harrison sped them across the water made the nausea return
with a vengeance and he swallowed hard against bile. The only
thing that kept Denny from throwing up was Steven's steady grip
on his arm and the fact Steven would kill him later. It occurred to
Denny that he was sitting in just about the exact spot where Brad
Flaherty had bloodied the deck, and he forced that thought away
with a vengeance.

They reached the *Agana* without running into any other boats.
Bud dropped anchor and Harrison changed into a wet suit.

"Sorry, we didn't bring you one," he said to Steven as he tossed
him a BCD.

"Someone want to tell me what we're diving for?" Steven asked.

"Piece of equipment," Bud said. "Heavy enough that it'll take both of you to haul it up. Remember that I'm going to be right here with this gun and your brother. You screw anything up, he'll pay for it."

Steven pulled on the vest. "I don't screw up."

Denny wanted to tell him to be careful. The *Agana* was treacherous enough in daytime, and she'd be a lot more unforgiving in total darkness. He didn't know anyone who'd ever dived the wreck at night. Also, Harrison couldn't be trusted. But Steven knew that already. Denny feared that once Steven went overboard he'd never see him again, and he started to freak out.

"Don't go," he said. "Stay here."

Steven squeezed Denny's shoulder. "It's okay. I'll be right back."

Moments later he and Harrison went over the side.

Bud said, "They'll be back soon."

Denny tried to track the time in his head. The *Agana* was sixty feet down. Steven and Harrison could descend quickly enough, but Tristan's pictures hadn't been clear on the equipment's exact location. They could spend just about an hour searching the bottom, fighting the currents and other underwater hazards, before doing a normal ascent. But they could be back a lot sooner than an hour, and somehow he had to neutralize Bud before that.

It helped that Bud was dividing his attention between Denny and the marine radio, listening for trouble. But the pistol stayed steadily aimed in Denny's direction, and he worried the Coast Guard Academy might not approve of him showing up with a bullet wound.

"More," Denny muttered, still playing at being addled. "What's more? More than what?"

"M-O-O-R," Bud said. "MOOR. It's a spy satellite that started to lose its orbit. NASA sent up a Delta rocket with a bigger satellite to capture it last week."

"And that's what crashed into the ocean?"

"Wasn't a crash," Bud said. "But it landed off target, and the payload got separated. That's what we're looking for."

Somewhere over Bud's shoulder, lights appeared—an approaching boat, slowly but steadily headed their way.

"You're not going to tell NASA you found it," he said. "Is that it? You're going to keep it for yourself?"

"Othello Industries is two days away from declaring bankruptcy," Bud said. "There's no future for the company. But there's a future for MOOR, once we deliver it to the people who made an offer on it."

The lights were growing closer. Denny thought back to what Claire had said about a business proposal she didn't feel comfortable taking. And Steven had seen Harrison kicked out of a moving van. "What people? Other governments?"

"You don't need to know," Bud said. "It can't help you."

The breeze kicked up again. Denny shivered and pulled his legs in tightly. He was readying himself to launch at Bud when the right moment came. He hoped he'd be able to do it and not just trip over himself.

An elderly woman's voice called out across the water as the other boat drew nearer. "Hello? Help! We need help!"

"Hell, no." Bud swung around and tucked the pistol into the back of his waistband. "You keep your mouth shut unless you want blood on your hands."

Denny swallowed hard. He recognized the boater. Sweet, harmless old Irma had a frantic expression on her face.

"My husband!" she said. "I think he's had a stroke, and our radio's out, and can you help?"

Ed was slumped on a bench, unmoving. A stroke was never good news, and Irma had picked the exact wrong person to ask for assistance.

"I don't know anything about strokes, ma'am," Bud said. "Our radio's out, too. It'd be best if you head straight to shore."

Denny imagined Irma turning away, and Bud shooting her in the back.

She started to cry. "The engine keeps stalling. I don't know about any of it—he takes care of everything. Can you show me? If he dies, I don't know what I'll do."

Bud sighed. "All right, hold on for one minute. Throw me that line, the one by your hand."

Irma tossed the line, but it fell short. She tried again. While Bud's attention was on the line, Denny rolled to his knees and prepared to tackle him. If he timed it right, if Bud didn't reach for his gun, if Irma stayed out of the way—

Bud swung around and pointed his finger at Denny. "You stay right there. Remember what I said."

Denny sat back, arms up.

"Please hurry," Irma said. "I don't know if he's breathing."

"I'm coming over," Bud said, and started to cross.

Irma held up her hand. It was kind of funny that she thought he needed her to steady him. Bud took it anyway and then slipped, or maybe Irma pulled him, or maybe the boat just rocked the wrong way. Denny wasn't sure. They went down on Irma's deck in a tangle of limbs.

A gunshot ripped through the air, making Denny flinch backward.

Oh, Irma, he thought miserably. *I got you killed.*

❖

Night diving was usually one of Steven's favorite activities. The underwater world was an entirely different and strange landscape at night. Like an alien planet only a few astronauts ever got to visit. Tonight, however, it was chalking up to be one of his least favorite experiences.

Number one, he wasn't wearing a wet suit and he was cold.

Number two, his dive "partner" was violent, untrustworthy, and unpredictable.

Number three, his brother was up on the boat as a hostage of someone else violent and unpredictable.

And oh, number four, the currents were even stronger than usual, reducing visibility and threatening to suck him away from the wreck.

Harrison hadn't skimped on the equipment—they each had a flashlight plus a backup LED strapped to their vests. He'd also attached a strobe LED to the bottom of Larry Gold's boat, so that when Steven looked up he could see exactly where it was. Harrison didn't seem intimidated by the size of the *Agana*, but he also was wearing a long knife strapped to his leg. If Bud had been telling the truth earlier, Harrison wouldn't stab him or sever his air hose until they had hauled the missing equipment to the surface.

Steven didn't think he or Denny would live very long once these guys had what they were after.

Once they reached bottom, the currents eased and visibility cleared. Harrison led the search. Slowly they coasted over the sand, separated by just a few feet, the beams of their flashlights intersecting as they swept back and forth. A spiny lobster skittered away from Steven's light, as did an enormous sea turtle. He thought that if Brad or Tristan were here they'd get some good shots.

Maybe "shot" wasn't the best word to think about right now. He hoped Denny wasn't doing anything stupid. Even without a big bump on your head, rushing the bad guy was a strategy of the last resort.

Twenty minutes sped by as they searched along the sea floor. Steven kept an eye on his watch and never let Harrison drift behind him. He was beginning to doubt they'd be able to find anything with just one dive and tried to figure out a way he could get the upper hand when they rose.

He wondered if he could kill Harrison, if it came to it.

Harrison lifted a hand. There, at the edge of his beam, was a battered metal globe that certainly looked like some kind of space junk. As they closed in on it, Steven couldn't see any markings or notations—just some nodules and seals and very few places for a handhold. It was larger than the component they'd recovered earlier and it was resting in several inches of sand. As they tugged it free he realized it probably weighed a hundred pounds or more.

Should have brought a winch, he thought.

Harrison had packed some strapping in his vest pockets. Within just a few minutes he'd improvised a sling they could use to balance the satellite between them and still hold on to their flashlights. They each had a loop to hold, with plenty of slack. Harrison motioned toward the surface, and they adjusted their BC vests to begin the ascent.

A plan started to take shape in Steven's head. He wasn't sure it would work, and if it failed Harrison would probably knife him, but he was out of other options.

His flashlight slipped out of his hand. He cursed behind his mask, pretending it was an accident, and reached past Harrison to grab for it.

Harrison yelled out something—*let it go*, probably.

Steven swung his end of the sling over Harrison's dive tank, looped it again, and let go.

Instantly the weight of the satellite tugged Harrison down into the depths. Harrison's flashlight fell away but the one on his tank sank quickly out of sight.

Steven turned off the light on his own tank.

Total darkness now.

No, not total. Peering upward, he saw the blinking LED on the bottom of Larry Gold's boat.

Steven wanted to race upward, but he couldn't. Not from sixty feet down, not unless he wanted nitrogen bubbles boiling in his blood. For the first time ever, he skipped the recommended safety stop at fifteen feet, though, and simply slowed himself more as the light drew nearer and nearer.

He surfaced near the bow, low and quiet. Another boat was alongside Larry's, and voices were murmuring. Denny, definitely, and a woman? A man who wasn't Bud?

Steven slid his tank off and let it sink. It wasn't his equipment, anyway. He circled around Larry's port side, away from the visitors.

"How long have they been down there?" the man was asking.

"A half hour at least," Denny said, worried. "Maybe more."

Steven knew that voice. Ed, the old NASA guy.

He reached up for the railing, and asked, "What's going on up here?"

Denny's face appeared above him, scrunched with worry. "Are you okay? Where's Harrison?"

Steven grinned at him. "Pull me up and I'll tell you."

He was halfway over the railing when a hand grabbed his ankle and yanked him downward. Steven yelped. He didn't lose grip of the railing, but it was close. Irma and Ed reached for him, grabbing at his arms.

Denny grabbed for a fishing net instead.

"Hell no," he said, and swung it over the side, past Steven, right into Jamie Harrison.

CHAPTER THIRTY-SIX

Denny was happily wrapped in two blankets, drinking hot chocolate Irma had fixed, determined not to move off the galley bench until he absolutely had to. Irma and Ed had a nice boat—a nice, warm, dry boat. Through the portholes he could see the Coast Guard sailors taking custody of Bud and Harrison. Bud had a bullet wound to his shoulder and Harrison had a bruised shoulder. He was lucky—Denny had been aiming the fishing net for his head.

Another boat pulled alongside. Denny knew the sound of the *Sleuth-hound* anywhere. He pushed back the blankets, ready to face the world, but Irma wagged her finger at him from the doorway.

"You stay right there," she said. "You have a concussion."

"I don't have a concussion," Denny protested.

A moment later she was leading Dad inside, with Brian and Sean close behind him. Dad looked wrecked.

"Twice in one week you do this to me," he said. "I'm going to have a heart attack just like Larry Gold."

"Not funny, Dad," Denny said.

Dad cupped Denny's head and peered closely at his eyes. "I agree. Not funny at all."

"Are you okay?" Brian asked. "They said you were hurt."

"I'm fine," Denny insisted.

Sean said, "You look green."

"It's the lighting," Denny said. "Steven's all banged up. Go fuss over him."

"I'll fuss over whoever I want," Dad said, but after a moment he went to check on Steven.

Brian slid onto the bench beside Denny. He looked like he needed a big fat hug. Or maybe Denny needed it, and he didn't care if Irma and Ed saw it or not. He leaned forward and let Brian wrap him in his arms. Brian smelled like sweat and salt, like something Denny wanted to get used to.

"I totally forgive you for dinner," Brian murmured shakily, and Denny laughed.

After a few minutes Denny told them he needed fresh air, and if his legs were a little unsteady as he stood up, he blamed the waves under the boat. Steven was sitting on a bench outside with an ice pack against his right knee. It didn't look too swollen. Yet.

"Had to be the same one," he complained.

Dad asked, "The same one as what?"

"Never mind," Steven said. "Hey, look, there's Denny with his head wound."

"I don't have a head wound," Denny said.

"Let the doctor decide," Dad retorted.

"Always a good idea," Ed said, from where he'd been talking to the Coast Guard lieutenant. "I'm a big believer in doctors. And fiber. And prune juice, when you get to be my age."

"I'd say your age is just fine," Irma told him, and gave him a brief kiss.

Dad said, "I think I'm a little unclear still on how you just happened to be around to save my sons."

Irma offered a secretive smile. "We heard the Coast Guard alert."

Ed said, "Fortuitous timing wins the day."

Dad stared at them skeptically. Denny was skeptical, too. He didn't think they were any ordinary retirees. Retired spies, maybe. Retired government agents. Retired heroes who'd indeed saved

Denny and Steven, and for that he was willing to let them keep any secret they wanted.

The Coast Guard was ready to leave. After a quick consultation, Dad decided to go back with them and make sure Bud and Harrison were properly jailed for the night. Dad tasked Brian with taking his sons back to land in the *Sleuth-hound* and seeing that they got to the hospital for a checkup.

"Don't let them talk you out of it," Dad said sternly. "Brian, you're in charge."

After Dad was gone, Sean said, "How come he's in charge? He's known me longer."

"Exactly because he's known you longer." Denny turned to Ed and Irma. "Thank you. For everything."

Irma ruffled his hair and Ed shook their hands.

"Take care, boys," he said. "I'd say 'stay out of trouble,' but that's probably not likely."

The trip back to Fisher Key was brief and quiet. Denny was dead tired and wanted to lie down, but he forced himself to stay upright. Steven's ice bag had melted and he flexed his knee tentatively, thoughtfully. The stars were a lovely blanket of lights over the sleeping island, and Denny was startled to see that it was almost two o'clock in the morning.

As they piled into Brian's mom's car, Brian said, "Okay, to the hospital."

"First we have to make a stop," Denny said.

Brian asked, "What? Where?"

Steven shared a look with Denny before saying, "Key West."

Sean turned around from the front seat. "Are you insane?"

"Black belt test," Denny said. "We promised."

Brian shook his head. "I promised your dad we'd go to the hospital."

"He'll shoot us if we don't," Sean added.

Steven said, "He didn't say which one. There's a hospital in Key West. We'll go there right after the test."

Sean threw his hands up in exasperation. "In case you haven't noticed, you both nearly got killed tonight!"

Denny leaned forward, reached through the seats, and took Brian's hand. "I know it's crazy, but it's important to us. We've been waiting for this for years. And it's the only chance we're going to have before everything ends this summer."

Brian said, "It's insane. I'm no karate expert, but neither of you is in any shape for a black belt test."

"We're fine," Denny said. "And if we're not, no foul. We just bow out."

Brian didn't say anything. But his expression was wavering, and Steven must have seen it, too.

Steven said, "We can be there in ninety minutes. Plenty of time to get a hot shower and some sleep and go to the hospital if Denny's head explodes."

"Not funny," Denny said.

Sean covered his face and groaned. "Your dad's totally going to shoot us."

Brian said nothing. Denny squeezed his fingers. This wasn't about being macho or pigheaded. It was about honoring a commitment and not letting douchebags like Bud and Harrison get in the way of dreams.

"Okay," Brian said, and he turned the ignition.

CHAPTER THIRTY-SEVEN

Steven was halfway through his Pinan Yodan kata when the dojo door opened and his father came in. Wearing his full uniform. Accompanied by Mom and Aunt Riza.

Dad did not look happy.

Busted, Steven thought to himself.

It shouldn't have thrown him off, but it did. He nearly flubbed the next block. But he kept going, because that's what you did in the middle of a black belt test with your sensei and his sensei judging every single move. You did the blocks and punches and steps as best you could, even when you were dead tired and your knee was aching and your father looked like he'd come to arrest you.

He didn't dare share a glance with Denny, who was kneeling by the side of the dojo waiting his turn. All Steven did was keep moving, breathing, using his body as both weapon and shield, fighting the imaginary foes the katas had been designed to fend off.

Sweat rolled into his eyes and the muscles in his legs trembled with fatigue, but he reached the end and bowed.

Silence now, except for the ceiling fans. Sensei Mike and Sensei Enji sat rock-still at the front of the room. Sensei Teresa stood nearby attentively. She looked a little sleepy, maybe because Steven had knocked on her door at five a.m. with a big favor to ask.

"We kind of need uniforms," he said. "And patches. And maybe a little breakfast. I promise we'll make it up to you."

From the doorway of her little cottage in Bahama Village, Teresa had stared at the ragtag collection in front of her: Steven, Denny, Sean, and Brian, none of them particularly rested after a painfully short catnap in the car.

"You're kidding me," she said.

But she came through for them, which Steven had counted on—she was a former Marine and that's what Marines did. She got on the phone and tracked down uniforms and tasked Sean and Brian with making bacon and eggs. Steven hadn't been able to eat much. Denny barely touched anything. But they both showered, drank black coffee, and took aspirin. Denny asked Teresa not to tell Sensei Mike anything about their arrival on her doorstep at five in the morning.

"I won't tell him, as long as you don't push yourselves too far," she'd said.

But how far was too far? Steven didn't know. He didn't even know what time it was because the only clock was in the office, well out of sight. He figured they'd been at this for three hours, maybe four, and maybe there'd be a break soon for the junior belts to go home, and the afternoon would be about weapons kata and then sparring.

Under normal circumstances, he'd enjoy sparring with Denny. Even on extremely little sleep, even after a night in which they both could have died.

Right now, though, he wasn't even sure Denny was going to get through the next kata.

Not that his brother was puking or weaving or doing anything obviously wrong. In fact, as Denny was called up for his Pinan Godan, everyone else probably thought he looked focused and steady. But under his tan he was pale, and his posture was too stiff, and he was clenching his fists in a way meant to hide the shaking of his hands.

"Pinan Godan," Denny announced, as required, and started.

Steven was supposed to be resting and staring at the floor, but he slid his gaze to Sensei Mike and Sensei Enji. Sensei Enji was as old as Steven had expected, but also shorter and stockier. His and Mike's expressions were both inscrutable. Instead of evaluating Denny's every move, they might just as well have been thinking about lunch or a movie they'd seen.

Denny did his left block and punch, followed by his right block and punch, and all his forward moves. When he reversed with a downward block he stumbled and almost lost his balance. He reversed again and nailed the rest of the blocks and punches, but when he ended he looked positively green.

Denny returned to the floor beside Steven.

"Do you want to stop?" Steven whispered.

"No," Denny muttered.

Steven was called up for Pinan Godan next. It took every ounce of concentration he had not to miss a move. His punches felt sluggish, his feet not as quick as they should be. He firmly ignored the fact that every eye in the dojo was watching him, including Mom and Dad. When he knelt afterward, he realized his knees were trembling.

Okay, maybe he needed a break, too.

Sensei Mike and Sensei Enji leaned their heads together for a brief consultation. Sensei Mike's gaze darted once to Denny, then twice. Sensei Teresa shuffled from one foot to the other uneasily. Steven didn't dare look toward the office because Dad might just take that as a sign to intervene.

"Pinan Dai," Sensei Mike said, and motioned for Steven and Denny to do it simultaneously.

Pinan Dai was all five of the pinan katas performed in one fluid sequence. Steven climbed to his feet. Denny was a little slower, but seemed fine enough until they got to the middle of the dojo floor. They were facing the front, about to begin, when he abruptly turned and whispered, "I can't."

Steven forgot all about his stance. "Yes, you can."

Denny's eyes were glassy. "I'm going to bow out. You keep going."

It was the smartest thing to do. Clearly Denny wasn't going to be able to finish. Steven had a much better chance of finishing out the day, or at least complete as much as he could. Just because they'd started karate together didn't mean they had to reach black belt at the same time. Being twins didn't mean crossing the finish line together.

Except it sort of did.

Steven turned to the front of the dojo and silently bowed to Sensei Mike and Sensei Enji. His face felt hot, and his heart pounded erratically. A murmur went through the students who were watching. From the corner of his eye he watched Denny bow as well.

Sensei Mike said immediately, "The testing is now concluded. Congratulations to you all."

Noise broke out as the students rose, the spectators emerged from the office, and some of the younger students started setting out food and drinks on a long table. Amidst the flurry of activity Steven tugged Denny away from the commotion. Inside the bathroom, they splashed themselves with cold water and drank water and Denny sat on the floor, exhausted.

"You're an idiot," Denny said. "Why'd you stop?"

"I was tired," Steven replied. "Sue me."

Denny shook his head. "You're never going to get anywhere in life unless I push you."

"Ha." Steven sat down beside him. "You're delusional."

Someone knocked. Sensei Teresa poked her head in and said, "You two okay?"

"Never better," Steven said.

"Good. Sensei Mike wants to see you."

Steven winced. Now they'd pay the price of disappointing Mike in front of his own teacher. Moments later, standing in Mike's private office with its pictures of Japan and famous martial artists, he tried to figure out how angry Mike was with them. But it was Sensei Enji who spoke, at length, in Japanese, while first eying Denny and then Steven from head to toe.

Sensei Mike said, "He says he would have enjoyed seeing you fight. That you're both strong in spirit and body."

Steven said, "We apologize for not finishing."

"It's my fault," Denny said.

"It's mine," Steven said firmly.

Sensei Enji said something else.

"He'll be back at Christmas," Sensei Mike translated. "He wants to see you both then, right here, to finish this test."

Steven was startled. "I thought he only came from Japan every ten years."

"He's retiring right here to Key West," Sensei Mike said. "Buying a condo over by the airport."

"Christmas," Sensei Enji said, heavily accented. "You here?"

Denny spoke for both of them. "Yes, we'll be here."

And then he sagged toward the floor, boneless and limp. It was a damn good thing Steven caught him before he hit his head on the corner of the desk.

"I think we might need that ambulance after all," Steven said.

CHAPTER THIRTY-EIGHT

I'm fine," Denny insisted, late that afternoon, as they climbed the steps to the apartment over the Bookmine. "I can sleep on the *Idle*."

Mom pointed to the sofa. "Right there, young man."

"I wouldn't argue with her," Dad said. "You missed it, but she's been lecturing you since we left the hospital."

Denny had missed it because he'd napped the entire drive back. Spending four hours in the emergency room hadn't been any fun at all. After x-rays and fluids and blood tests, the doctor had said he didn't have anything worse than a case of exhaustion and maybe a mild concussion.

"A wrench will do that," Steven had muttered, though not loud enough for Mom or Dad to hear.

Imprisoned on the sofa, fussed over with blankets and ice water and more blankets by Mom and Aunt Riza both, Denny asked, "Where's Steven?"

"Washing his truck," Dad said. "He's still mad that Jamie Harrison dumped it in the woods at Big Pine Key for the rangers to find. That's how we really knew you two were in trouble. Steven would never leave it, and you'd never piss him off by leaving it."

Steven came by a half hour later, sweaty and smelling like car wax. He plopped down in the armchair and said, "I hope that delicious smell is bunuelos."

Aunt Riza beamed. "For my favorite nephews."

"You've got to help me escape," Denny whispered.

Dad overheard and wagged his finger. "You're both staying here tonight, where we can keep an eye on you."

Steven asked. "Where? There's no beds."

"I've got some air mattresses on the way," Dad said.

"So not fair," Steven replied. "It's not like we asked for trouble."

Mom kissed the top of Steven's head. "But it finds you anyway."

Denny didn't want to stay overnight in the apartment. He wanted to go find Brian, and maybe they could go to sleep in that big comfy bed in Brian's room—though just that, sleep, because even if the calendar in his head were to start blinking 1 DAY LEFT with klaxon alarms and a whooping siren, he was too tired to even think about milestones tonight.

"In the morning we're all going up to Miami for Aunt Riza's party," Dad said. "And now that Steven's got his vision test all sorted out, it's going to be an even better party than it was before."

Denny was glad about Steven's test. More glad than he could even express, because now Steven wouldn't be flipping out about it every day. But the reminder of the party was like salt in a wound because of Brian. Brian, who'd driven down to Key West with them in the middle of the night and stayed in the dojo for the test and come to the hospital, too.

Mom said, "What's wrong, Denny?"

Everyone looked at him.

"Nothing," he said. But then, because it really wasn't nothing, he said, "I don't feel right going without Brian. He's my boyfriend and I want him to be there."

Mom shifted her gaze to Aunt Riza, who was standing at the kitchen counter with a spatula in hand while dinner sizzled in the pan in front of her.

"He and Sean did save your lives," Dad pointed out from the

tiny card table. "If they hadn't figured out and told me that Larry's boat was gone, I wouldn't have been able to put out that alert that Ed and Irma heard."

Aunt Riza stirred dinner. "I don't approve of boys kissing boys."

"I know," Denny said. "I'm not asking you to."

She made a humming noise. "Then again, he is a nice young man. And it is your party."

He waited a minute, but she said nothing more. "Does that mean yes, he can come?"

"It means dinner is ready," she said, with a small smile. "Come and eat."

Denny rose and gave her a hug. She was short enough to fit under his chin and light enough to pick up and squeeze.

"Put me down!" she squeaked.

"Thanks," he said.

"You're still sleeping here tonight," Dad said.

Steven asked, "If he gets to bring his boyfriend, can I bring my girlfriend?"

"Is there a girl on this island who isn't mad at you?" Denny asked.

Steven reached for his phone. "Let's find out."

CHAPTER THIRTY-NINE

Brian woke Monday morning to a ringing phone. He ignored it. If it was Denny, he'd call Brian's cell. If it was Sean, saying that another tree had fallen on Denny (or some other improbable disaster), it would also be on the cell phone. The sun was shining and the air-conditioning was glorious and Brian was perfectly content to lay in bed, dozing, thinking of Denny and the day they'd had yesterday in Miami: beautiful weather, a great going-away party, kissing under a blazing red sunset sky.

And today they were supposed to go out on Denny's boat, just the two of them, out to Bardet Key. Overnight. Alone. No kidnappers, spies, missing satellites, or any other kind of trouble.

Brian smiled into his pillow.

Mom knocked on his door. "Honey, you awake?" she asked, and cracked it open.

"Yeah, sure," he said, and rolled over to face her.

"That's the financial aid office on the line," she said. "They want to talk to us both about your tuition package."

Brian instantly sat up. "Is it good news or bad news?"

"I don't know yet," she said.

Brian stood up, grabbed a shirt to pull on, and tried to quell the uneasy roll of his stomach.

"It's okay," Mom said, squeezing his shoulder. "We'll figure it out, right?"

"Sure," he said. They'd figure it out. His whole future, waiting on the other end of the phone line. He took a deep breath and followed her down the hall, hoping his dreams weren't about to come crashing down around him.

Don't miss Sam Cameron's next
Fisher Keys Adventure

The Missing Juliet

Coming from Soliloquy,
a division of Bold Strokes Books

Turn the page to read a preview…

THE MISSING JULIET

I hope you realize we're trespassing on federal property,"
Sean whispered, pushing a palm frond away from his
face. "The Truman House is a historic landmark!"

"Shut up," Robin suggested as she kept crawling through
the bushes. She didn't care if they got arrested. A stint in jail
was nothing compared to meeting Juliet Francine for just
one minute. Those perfect blue eyes, crystal bright. That
strawberry-blond hair and long, loose curls, perfect for running
fingers through. Sweet pink lips that would probably taste like
summer strawberries—

Not for the first time, Robin realized how ridiculous it
was to daydream about someone she'd only seen in movies
and on TV. This was all nothing but a silly teenage crush.
She should be home, editing new YouTube videos protesting
cyberbullying and gender discrimination. Someone had to
speak up against the injustices of the world. Instead, she was
getting her favorite lesbian pride T-shirt all dirty and risking a
permanent arrest record if they charged her as an adult.

Love was crazy.

Sean complained, "I think this is poison ivy. If I get a rash,
you're paying for the cream."

Robin elbowed him in the side to shut him up and then dropped to the ground. Sean followed. There, through the ferns, they could see cast and crew members standing under a green tent about forty feet away. Sulking in a chair with his name on it was Liam Norcott, Hollywood's favorite bad boy. He had tousled blond hair and pouty red lips and a reputation for trouble.

"Michael, if she's not here in the next sixty seconds, I'm going back to my trailer," he said angrily as he texted on his phone. "This is ridiculous."

Not as ridiculous as his diesel-belching double-decker trailer parked in the street nearby, Robin thought. Liam Norcott was all looks and no talent.

"I'm going to die," Sean said into Robin's ear. "I've had a crush on him since I was twelve years old."

"He's an idiot," Robin whispered back. "Look for Juliet."

The director, Michael Lake, turned away and spoke hurriedly into his cell phone. A makeup girl tried to dust Liam's nose, but he shooed her away. Some actresses wearing clothing from the 1940s rehearsed their lines. A movie set was sort of like high school, Robin realized—a lot of people waiting around for the interesting parts to happen. A mosquito dug into her arm, but she swatted it away. She could wait all day if she had to, and she wasn't going to let the heat or bugs or anything else get in the way.

"Michael!" a voice called out, and there she was far down the path—Juliet Francine, tall and pretty and clutching a note in her hands. Robin's heart started beating thunderously fast. She was going to do it. She was going to step out of hiding and come face-to-face with the girl of her dreams, and not be a creepy stalker fan but someone Juliet would think was cool, and maybe she'd give her an autograph, and then maybe they'd have iced coffee and talk a lot—

But wait. That wasn't Juliet at all. It was her older sister Karen, also strawberry-blond and slender, but not quite as pretty. Karen rushed to the director and thrust a piece of paper into his hands.

"What?" Michael Lake asked as he scanned it. "Is this a joke?"

"Is what a joke?" Liam demanded. He snatched the paper away and read it quickly. "Oh, come on! It's the oldest publicity stunt in Hollywood!"

Karen Francine turned on him, her face pale and hands shaking. "It's no joke!" she said. "Juliet's been kidnapped!"

About the Author

A Navy veteran, Sam Cameron spent several years serving in the Pacific and along the Atlantic coast. Her transgender, romance, and science fiction novels have been recognized for their wit, inventiveness, and passion. She holds an MFA in creative writing and currently teaches college in Florida.

Soliloquy Titles From Bold Strokes Books

The Secret of Othello by Sam Cameron. Florida teen detectives Steven and Denny risk their lives to search for a sunken NASA satellite—but under the waves, no one can hear you scream… (978-1-60282-742-4)

Andy Squared by Jennifer Lavoie. Andrew never thought anyone could come between him and his twin sister, Andrea… until Ryder rode into town. (978-1-60282-743-1)

Sara by Greg Herren. A mysterious and beautiful new student at Southern Heights High School stirs things up when students start dying. (978-1-60282-674-8)

Boys of Summer, edited by Steve Berman. Stories of young love and adventure, when the sky's ceiling is a bright blue marvel, when another boy's laughter at the beach can distract from dull summer jobs. (978-1-60282-663-2)

Street Dreams by Tama Wise. Tyson Rua has more than his fair share of problems growing up in New Zealand—he's gay, he's falling in love, and he's run afoul of the local hip-hop crew leader just as he's trying to make it as a graffiti artist. (978-1-60282-650-2)

me@you.com by K.E. Payne. Is it possible to fall in love with someone you've never met? Imogen Summers thinks so because it's happened to her. (978-1-60282-592-5)

Swimming to Chicago by David-Matthew Barnes. As the lives of the adults around them unravel, high school students Alex and Robby form an unbreakable bond, vowing to do anything to stay together—even if it means leaving everything behind. (978-1-60282-572-7)

Speaking Out edited by Steve Berman. Inspiring stories written for and about LGBT and Q teens of overcoming adversity (against intolerance and homophobia) and experiencing life after "coming out." (978-1-60282-566-6)

365 Days by K.E. Payne. Life sucks when you're seventeen years old and confused about your sexuality, and the girl of your dreams doesn't even know you exist. Then in walks sexy new emo girl, Hannah Harrison. Clemmie Atkins has exactly 365 days to discover herself, and she's going to have a blast doing it! (978-1-60282-540-6)

Cursebusters! by Julie Smith. Budding psychic Reeno is the most accomplished teenage burglar in California, but one tiny screw-up and poof!—she's sentenced to Bad Girl School. And that isn't even her worst problem. Her sister Haley's dying of an illness no one can diagnose, and now she can't even help. (978-1-60282-559-8)

Who I Am by M.L. Rice. Devin Kelly's senior year is a disaster. She's in a new school in a new town, and the school bully is making her life miserable—but then she meets his sister Melanie and realizes her feelings for her are more than platonic. (978-1-60282-231-3)

Sleeping Angel by Greg Herren. Eric Matthews survives a terrible car accident only to find out everyone in town thinks he's a murderer—and he has to clear his name even though he has no memories of what happened. (978-1-60282-214-6)

Mesmerized by David-Matthew Barnes. Through her close friendship with Brodie and Lance, Serena Albright learns about the many forms of love and finds comfort for the grief and guilt she feels over the brutal death of her older brother, the victim of a hate crime. (978-1-60282-191-0)

The Perfect Family by Kathryn Shay. A mother and her gay son stand hand in hand as the storms of change engulf their perfect family and the life they knew. (978-1-60282-181-1)

Father Knows Best by Lynda Sandoval. High school juniors and best friends Lila Moreno, Meryl Morganstern, and Caressa Thibodoux plan to make the most of the summer before senior year. What they discover that amazing summer about girl power, growing up, and trusting friends and family more than prepares them to tackle that all-important senior year! (978-1-60282-147-7)